TARGETED INNOCENT

DONNA BAXTER

Publishing Coordinator – Sharon Kizziah-Holmes

Paperback-Press
an imprint of A & S Publishing
Paperback Press, LLC.
Springfield, Missouri

ISBN -13: 978-1-964559-48-3

ACKNOWLEDGMENTS

Targeted Innocent – a "one-in-a-million" story – could never have been written if it had not been for several dedicated people who could see the truth.

One who stood out was Kansas City Attorney Michael G. Newbold who took the case, then followed through to a final affirmative decision in the Washington, DC, Equal Employment Opportunity investigation.

This book would never have been published if it were not for encouragement from my editor William Tatum for whom I am deeply appreciative. He had no prior knowledge of the events but believed the story should be told.

I can't say enough to express my appreciation to the Bureau of Prisons, Dept. of Justice and medical center staff/employees who served as union representatives, EEO counselors and investigators. All involved said they had never seen a case like this.

Special thanks to my coworkers at the medical center, especially to those who gave testimonies. They were also helpful and encouraging throughout the entire ordeal.

And finally, but not least, my family who at the time knew nothing of what I was going through but said later they knew something was wrong.

                   __ Donna Baxter

FOREWORD

It was different back then -- Donna Baxter would tell you -- when a woman in a mostly male work environment had to deal every day with sexism, chauvinism and second-class status.

Even if a capable woman could hold her own working alongside the boys' club, she might never know when a jerk would emerge from the pack, rise through the ranks or show up from another office and become a tormentor or worse.

The federal prison system was not populated with men of ill intent but it took only one misogynistic manager to turn her satisfying career into a daily dose of hell.

Donna's story might have been different after the rise of the Me-Too Movement and growing numbers of women in positions of authority in the work world. But for her it took nerve and eventually the willingness to use the legal system to address the abuse and threats of a mean-spirited supervisor who expected subservience as much as office efficiency.

An apparent attempt to sabotage her workplace was the final straw that drove her from the job, but a supportive union system and a good lawyer helped her recover.

Here's a story of resilience and resolve.

___ William Tatum, editor

ABOUT THE STORY

Targeted Innocent is about a woman who realized she was working with people who apparently cared very little for human life. They allegedly were willing to blow up a hospital building full of patients and employees to get back at her for refusing an evil-minded misogynist's advances. She was forced to deal with circumstances that no one should ever have to face.

This story is true. It happened in a federal prison hospital several years ago. Much can be told now that the statute of limitations is long gone. All names were changed and fiction was used in a few places where needed for continuity.

Hundreds of thousands of complaints are filed each year in Washington, DC, by federal employees. Investigative records show that only 12 out of each 100 complaints ever reach arbitration. And of each 12, only one (1) wins and receives a settlement. Targeted Innocent is about one of the few that came out on top.

_ Donna Baxter

CHAPTER 1

DISASTER

R ed and blue emergency lights are common at any hospital, but so many flashing in the early hours at the medical prison puzzled employees arriving for the day.

As they got closer, it became clear something horrible had happened. Ambulances were loading and leaving with the injured. The main building at the federal prison hospital was in ruins. One wall was left standing.

"An explosion," an officer told Kay Richards as she arrived for work. "Looks like it was in the west end basement."

One of the first to arrive, Kay made her way to a police car where other shocked workers were gathered, everyone sobbing, clinging to each other and trying to understand. Agonized concern for those known to have been working that night could be heard.

Almost everyone working the midnight shift was seriously injured or dead, as were about 300 inmate patients.

Things became muddled as Kay started toward her office in another building. When a policeman called to her and demanded she get into his squad car, she realized she was under suspicion and began to run through the halls. He was catching up. Run… run… run… He grabbed her. She screamed.

Suddenly Kay sat straight up in bed. It was 2:10 a.m. Afraid to move and dripping with sweat, she reached over to wake her husband.

"One Building's gone… all gone," she cried. "Everyone's dead. All of them. They tried to arrest me."

He assured her that nothing had happened, and it was all a dream, but she lay awake. Finally, she got up to check the TV for news about an explosion at the federal prison hospital. Nothing.

But it was all so real.

She was relieved to find all the buildings intact when she got to work. Sitting at her desk, she could not get the dream off her mind.

Out loud, she asked herself, "Was it dream? A premonition? Or a warning?"

CHAPTER 2

THE WORLD TURNED UPSIDE DOWN

About 18 months later.

With keys in the ignition, Kay sat staring at the brick and concrete edifice across the parking lot. In the mid-morning sunlight, its menacing white dome glaring down at her.

Inside, a man who deserved all the hate she could muster, was probably drinking coffee with his buddies at that very moment. The omni-powerful good ol' boy system, deeply rooted and unmovable, had won again. She leaned her head against the steering wheel and wept.

A few minutes later she leaned back against the seat, physically and emotionally drained.

Previous supervisors had always treated her with

respect and given her excellent reviews. She believed she could outlast that evil man if she hung in there and continued to do her job to the best of her ability. If she did not give in to him, she thought his attitude toward her would change.

She asked herself, "Why is this man so different? Why did he have to come here? Am I being punished or just tested?"

Nothing about it made any sense. Her career, self-esteem... everything... had been destroyed.

Her thoughts drifted back almost two years...

The 20-minute drive to work from her sons' school gave Kay time to contemplate the day ahead. She had been employed at the United States Medical Center for Federal Prisoners in Springfield, Missouri, for 13 years. The institution, opened in 1933, confined about 1,100 inmates.

Inside a perimeter fence about a half mile wide, a cluster of buildings connected by underground tunnels form a square around a large recreation yard.

About 700 people worked there, an ethnic mix from every state in the union. The locals are easily distinguished by their soft, but distinct, Ozarks southern drawl. Personal aspirations range from "Yuppies" who see the institution as a career steppingstone to locals satisfied to work one job until they retired.

The light-hearted conversation while waiting in line to pick up keys always started off the workday on a positive note. Kay also enjoyed the stimulating half mile walk back to the Education Department in "8 Building." That morning the tunnels were practically empty, foot traffic impeded by a 7:30 general staff meeting.

Kay was administrative assistant to the supervisor of education, and she liked her job. The only woman in the department, she was responsible for the office and institution print shop. She supervised several inmate workers and was "liaison" between Education and other departments.

James Datema had been her supervisor for five years. The 50-year-old Washington state native claimed to be "100 percent Dutch and proud of it." He was a large well-built handsome man with a prominent moustache. His jovial disposition and humor made him a pleasure to work for. He joked and cut up with subordinates but maintained authority, was fair and respected. "Probably the best boss we'll ever have around here," was the usual summary of Jim.

As they walked toward the meeting, Kay thought how lucky she was to be working with a congenial group. Everyone cooperated and appreciated each other. Besides Jim and Kay, there were several teachers including Dan Williams, Earl Norman and Don Douglas as well as recreation supervisor Ben Byerly and his recreation specialists.

Today's meeting was to include Jim's presentation to Kay of a commendation for superior service.

The award was long overdue and much deserved, he had told her, and he had tried to get her grade level raised to reflect the rating given the position by the Regional Office a few years earlier. But the Medical Center administration continually refused approval, giving the "bottom line" as the reason.

Deep down, she felt it was because she was a woman.

"Seems like only those in management get much attention when it comes to the real awards and raises," Jim told her.

Dan also congratulated Kay and quipped, "What really did it was that chocolate cake she baked you for your birthday. Right, Boss?"

At 65, Dan was the department father figure. He reminded Kay of her own dad with his dry humor and caring attitude. He always knew how to handle any situation. Distinguished looking, tall and lean with a full head of gray hair, he had a huge vocabulary and cracked everyone up with his workplace poetry.

Kay enjoyed the kidding and "hard time" from her co-workers. It was like having several brothers. But little did they know then, the tranquility was destined to be short-lived.

Jim was past 50 and had completed 20 years of service so he was eligible for retirement. He enjoyed his job and wanted to work a few more years, but it was clear that someone higher-up was forcing him out.

On his last day, he said the new man was lucky to be getting such a good group and added that Kay had been a good assistant, and he appreciated her dedication.

"When your new boss arrives, Kay, keep the office running just as smooth for him as you have for me."

CHAPTER 3

THE SIEGE BEGINS

Dan was the only person in the department who had ever met Karl Greiner. They had attended a weeklong seminar several years earlier, and Dan remembered him as an egotistical "know-it-all" who monopolized discussions and interrupted instructors with his own opinions.

"I didn't appreciate his attitude then and if he hasn't drastically changed, I don't think he'll be a nice person to work for now," Dan said.

But Kay was pleased when an assistant in the Human Resource Office asked her to come to the front and escort Greiner to Education. The half-mile walk would give them a chance to start getting acquainted, she thought.

The new boss looked familiar, a dead ringer for

Peter Graves in the old "Mission Impossible" TV series. He had short-cropped gray-blond hair, was of average build, about six feet tall and appeared to be about 50 years old. He was neat and well-groomed in a pinstriped shirt, light blue tie and navy slacks. He was solemn almost to the point of looking sour, but there was no immediate clue to his true personality.

Walking through the tunnels, it was immediately obvious that Greiner was not interested in conversation or even civility.

To try to break the ice, Kay asked if his family was settled into their new home. He mumbled something inaudible.

She tried again, but he seemed annoyed and said he had three daughters in high school.

Kay had sons that same age and said it must have been difficult for his girls, especially the oldest, to leave their school and friends.

His is eyes fixed on the hallway ahead, Greiner snapped, "It doesn't make one damn bit of difference if they wanted to come here or not."

When the department closed for lunch, staff gathered in Kay's office to get acquainted. Right out of the blue and in front of the others, Karl asked Kay her grade level.

When she answered, Greiner looked down his nose and said in a cold haughty voice, "What I have in mind for *you* is a general secretary. I don't *need* an administrative assistant."

Right after lunch he asked Kay into the privacy of his office to "discuss" things.

He first asked who evaluated her performance,

another question to which he already knew the answer and motioned to a chair directly across the desk from him.

"Sit down right there," he said.

Relaxing a bit, he leaned back in his executive chair behind the large desk, fingers clasped behind his head and gave her a very intense look. A slight grin crossed his face, but his tone of voice remained flat and matter of fact.

"Your only purpose here is to please me and if you want a good evaluation, I am the only person you are to make happy."

Kay knew from management training that a statement like that, or anything that can be construed as sexual harassment, is an absolute "no-no" for a supervisor to say.

Karl had invited Kay to proposition him if she cared about a good evaluation.

Law and the "#MeToo" movement notwithstanding, she did not believe he would press the issue, but nothing could have been further from the truth. Karl had nothing but contempt for Kay, that much was clear, but why?

Because she had ignored his advances? Or did he just resent the fact that she was a person respected by her peers? A woman, no less.

"Maybe I remind him of someone from his past," she thought. "Maybe it's my small size or personality. Or maybe because I have sons and he has daughters. One thing's for sure, he places no value whatsoever on me as a human being."

Soon after Karl arrived, there was a mandatory week of training for supervisors on a new progressive discipline policy. It covered degrees of punishment for employee misconduct from a verbal reprimand to termination, depending on the offense and number of previous disciplinary actions.

Kay had no idea that policy soon would become a major part of her life.

Her satisfying work world was on a rapid slide toward hell. Not allowing herself to see what was really happening, she believed that somehow, she was to blame and kept telling herself that if she did a good job and remained patient, Karl would change. They could work together as a team like she and Jim had.

That expectation was shattered when Dan told her of a conversation he'd had with a supervisor in another department, a longtime acquaintance of Karl's.

After the other man said that he hoped he would never have to use the new policy, Karl stated without hesitation, "Well, I *intend* to use it."

"Why? Got a problem?"

"Yeah. I've given that bitch every chance to conform and be a team player. Broads don't have any goddamn business working inside prisons. Don't need any of 'em. Ought to fire the whole bunch."

Kay's translation: "She wouldn't give in to me so she's history."

The conversation spread through the institution "rumor mill," but Dan immediately repeated it to Kay. "He also told me Karl is a snake and we should watch out for him," he added.

At first, she ignored a "gut feeling" about Karl,

but now intuition was waving a red flag. Correctional employees develop and learn to heed that strong "sixth sense," but nothing could prepare her for what was coming.

Karl was constantly on her case, no matter what she did or said.

The inmate grapevine was also abuzz with tales of Karl. Inmates always become aware of an amazing amount of scuttlebutt about what goes on inside, and outside, a prison even though employees are forbidden to discuss personal matters with or in the presence of inmates.

Prisoners were overheard saying that Karl "ran around" where he used to work and that his wife and kids had "run off" at least once. They called him "mean, cold, indifferent, uncaring."

One new arrival, on learning Karl was in charge of inmate education, shook his head in disgusted disbelief, "I thought I was through with Greiner when they transferred me out of that last joint. But no-o-o!" he lamented. "Who's the first person I see when I get here? Greiner!"

Kay's personal rule on how to handle those who do not act in a professional manner was to not change her attitude toward *them* at all, but her philosophy had met its match with Karl. He never missed a chance to ridicule or belittle her. During one casual conversation with another individual, she mentioned a night class that evening.

Karl butted in and resounded, "I don't give a goddamn what you're doing or your goddamned blankety blank course!"

He could not even stand for anyone *else* to

acknowledge her presence. Was it because she's a woman? He probably hates his own mother, she thought.

The local employees' union knew of several previous incidents at other prisons involving problems Karl had with women employees and inmates' wives. He had been downgraded at least three times with disciplinary transfers. To avoid termination all this time, he must have had friends or influence in high places in the bureau.

There have always been the "ladder climbers" who embrace a certain attitude: Take whatever you need; step on whoever or whatever gets in your way. Weaker individuals, especially women and those less enlightened or influential, are for your use and convenience.

This description certainly fit Greiner. Kay had never met anyone so cold.

In the institution print shop, Kay handled jobs on a "first come, first served" basis except for special requisitions from the warden. On his third day, Karl had ordered that from that point on, all printing must go through *him* for approval. But he then allowed orders to lay for days before even looking at them, slowing output of the print shop to a snail's pace.

Kay had no idea what Karl was talking about when he burst through the office door, leaned over her desk and yelled right in her face. "Don't you *ever again* refer calls from line staff to me about printing or anything else! *Is that clear?* I will *not* talk to line officers! I only speak to *other* department heads!" Apparently, someone had inquired directly to him about a printing order.

The fit regarding the phone call lasted about five minutes. Then he turned on a completely different personality, became quiet and changed his tone of voice and the subject.

"I *am* kind of unique in view of my grade, you know. I'm actually under the warden but if the associate warden told me to do something, I guess I'd have to do it even through we're the same grade level."

At that moment, Kay realized how erratic his behavior was and that he was obsessed with grade levels, which represent authority – and power.

Whenever he leaned over her desk, his face so close she could feel his breath, and shook his forefinger two inches from her nose, it was intimidating. And Kay couldn't understand what he was mad about.

Simple answers to his questioning brought wild accusations.

And the never-ending refrain, "You aren't making me happy yet."

"What in creation am I going to do? Why won't he leave me alone?" she prayed after Karl had been her boss for only a short time. It seemed a lifetime.

One morning he did not show until after his daily three-hour coffee "confab" with the good ol' boys. When he stormed into Kay's office, he straight-out demanded, "What in hell is this contract employee doing with a mailbox alongside *staff*?"

He was referring to a registered nurse who conducted biweekly classes for diabetics and chronically ill prisoners. She picked up doctors' referrals and correspondence in the office and Kay handled her timecard and contract.

Karl had already ordered that there be no collection boxes or files for inmates which made it very inconvenient to organize and assign work to them each day.

Karl's orders were always given in a vague, hateful and derogatory manner. Kay never knew if what he said would be standing an hour later, let alone the next day, or if he would simply deny he had ever given the order.

Kay began to go out of her way to avoid Karl. She got a sick feeling in the pit of her stomach every time she saw him.

She was eager to oblige when he asked for a detailed description of the filing system used for education records. She had been commended on her files in the last regional audit.

She explained her detailed and rational system. His face remained expressionless.

"From now on," he said, "all hospital men are also to have files, and every outgoing inmate is to have one too even if it's totally empty. And that includes all those leaving today and tomorrow."

She started to explain reasons that would be impractical, but Karl interrupted, called her argumentative and yelled, "You follow my orders! I'll show those other bastards how an education file is supposed to look!"

Several time-consuming computer retrievals were needed for each new inmate record, and several hundred more files would immediately be needed. It was all so – *impossible*! She covered her face to hide her tears.

Right then and there, she came to a firm conclusion, "This is a no-win situation. I have to take steps to protect myself."

CHAPTER 4

KNEE DEEP IN ALLIGATORS

After work Kay recorded the events of the day during the drive to pick up her boys at school. It was fresh in her mind and she would later transcribe it in a journal.

Years of Equal Employment Opportunity involvement had taught her to document and date everything that could be construed as harassment, even if it seemed insignificant at the time.

In Karl's short time at the prison it had become clear to Kay that she had a serious problem. Her best efforts to get along were unsuccessful. The situation just grew progressively worse.

He had given Kay an impossible mandate regarding the education files.

Few empty folders were on hand since the

customized multi-sectional files were recycled as the inmate population changed. Other departments in the institution used different styles and none were available locally. Karl demanded that no manila or other temporary folder be used in the meantime.

Kay special ordered 800, and a few were obtained from education departments at other institutions.

One call was to Karl's last duty station, the federal prison at Leavenworth, Kansas.

Kay's counterpart at Leavenworth, Bev Wilson, promised to send along some folders and after a few minutes of conversation asked her, "Well, how *is* old Greiner?"

Her tone and expression told Kay they had a lot in common.

"I need to ask you something," Kay said. "Does he have a problem with women?"

Bev told a similar story to what Kay had endured since Karl became her boss. They had much to share so they exchanged home phone numbers.

Bev had filed an EEO complaint against Karl but dropped it after he left.

Union representatives at Leavenworth told the medical center union about Karl's big-time problems with women employees and with inmates' wives. They also said that Karl was told when he was downgraded and transferred from that prison that "if he went down to Springfield and kept his nose clean, he might get to retire."

Management rarely accepted prisoners' word over that of staff so Karl felt free to harass Kay in front of a classroom full of inmates. In fact, he obviously enjoyed it. He was also confident the male employees would back him.

An example of this: Karl walked by Kay just as she made a passing remark to a co-worker about her full wastebasket. This brought down a thorough threshing on the spot for discussing work in front of inmates. Everyone was shocked because nothing against regulations had been said while Karl, himself, was violating the same policy that also specifically forbids supervisors from criticizing subordinates in the presence of inmates, staff or other employees.

A few minutes later, the same prisoners listened while Karl and teacher Earl Norman discussed departmental procedures. The prisoners looked at Kay and rolled their eyes. They know employee conduct regulations better than some staff.

Several inmates volunteered written eyewitness accounts. A middle-aged first offender said to Kay, "I've been out in the business world for over thirty years and seen a lot of bad behavior, but I've *never* observed *anything* like the insults, put-downs, disrespect and just plain mean treatment – especially of a woman in the office – the way Mr. Greiner and Mr. Norman treat you."

Being firm but fair, Kay had always had a good rapport with prisoners. Word rapidly spread among the inmates that she was getting the shaft. They related since most of them feel the same way regarding their incarceration. One day, she realized that they had become her self-appointed guardians. At least one education worker was always present in the study room adjoining the office.

Never a day went by without Karl's verbal abuse. After repeating everything already covered in previous thrashings, he would add new charges. The files kept coming up as if there was anything she could do about that. He always included "not following orders." How was she to know which version of his demands he wanted carried out? It did not matter what she did.

Then Karl took away all her inmate clerks. "No inmate is to set foot in this office to help you! You are to receive no help in here from anybody. *Understand?"*

To top it off, he fired the best clerk she ever had – a trustee who could be counted on to do a job correctly without being watched constantly. The inmate had witnessed much and had the courage to tell Karl that Kay did not deserve what he (Greiner) and Earl were doing to her.

Dan told her the teachers were all informed that if they assisted her in any way, they would be disciplined.

"I don't care what he says," he said. "I'll help you at any time and in any way I can. He's being ridiculous. No matter what, I'll still back you to the end."

He added that he was old enough to retire and was "only one bad day away from it."

Her voice quivered. "Dan, it seems his mission is to make it impossible for me to work, then yell at me about it. He acts like he wants to get me fired."

"You've got it, Kay."

He backed up this statement by revealing a conversation he had overheard between Karl and

Earl the evening before. They were discussing that they needed "to get rid of Kay."

"I want to warn you their plan is to put you in a compromising position that will cause you to lose your job. I guess they felt safe talking in my presence."

Dan paused a moment, then became even more serious. He looked her straight in the eye and said, "Kay, these are *evil* men."

Cold chills ran up her spine.

When Earl first came to the Medical Center, he was a bit full of himself but otherwise appeared to be okay. He seemed eager, cooperative and interested in the students. But his personality and attitude toward Kay changed drastically after Karl arrived.

Kay thought it strange that Earl carried on as a single man with no apparent plans to have his wife and two children join him. He even told an inmate he was going to divorce his "fat wife."

Earl had lived near Chicago until his first prison job about two years before coming to the Medical Center. In his early forties, his career was stalled and his desire to climb the ladder at any cost made him eager when given the opportunity to conspire with, or for, Karl.

A small man with sharp features and receding hairline, Earl had a sly sneaky demeanor. Childish stunts to annoy Kay were more of a nuisance at first than anything else, but his constant surveillance and meddling were as unnerving as Karl's sudden appearance.

At first, Kay did not give it much thought but

almost every time she returned to the office, Earl was at her desk using her computer. One morning he was there when she arrived an hour before his usual duty hour. She asked how long he needed to be there.

In a bratty tone, he said, "Kay, if you complain to me, I'll just tell Karl and then you'll get it."

Karl's tireless tirades were like a broken record, plus asinine statements like, "I've been trying to figure this all out. Is it stubbornness, belligerence, disobedience, forgetfulness, stupidity or just plain bullheadedness? I've had nothing but trouble from you ever since I got here. This whole department is going to hell and *you* are totally to blame!"

After one tongue-lashing, Kay decided that she could no longer handle it alone. Her friend Glenda Potter, an EEO counselor, was the institution data coordinator. In her late thirties, she was jovial, quick-witted, fun to be around.

Kay felt eyes on her constantly and Karl seemed to be aware of her every move. At work, she was careful to see Glenda only when she was officially scheduled to be keying data.

It was hard at first to confide in her friend. She was afraid Glenda would think she had somehow caused Karl's behavior. She almost broke down several times while sharing details of Karl's abuse and accusations.

When Kay repeated his statement that she was fully to blame for the department's demise, Glenda quipped, "Boy, you sure went to hell in a hurry!" Kay had to laugh.

But quickly, "Listen to me, Kay. You are in no

way to blame for this."

It helped to have another woman in whom to confide. She had not talked about her situation with anyone except Dan who witnessed much of the abuse.

Fear of condemnation is a symptom in a person being abused or under a great deal of stress. Tension from keeping everything bottled up causes more anxiety.

Kay felt the subject was altogether too painful to share with her husband believing he'd also think it was her own fault. It was not a suitable subject for discussion with her sons either.

Word got out about the turmoil in Education. Kay realized almost everyone was rallying behind her. Concerned staff, management personnel and even inmates were cheering her on even though they were helpless to intervene. People would pat her on the shoulder or voice encouragement. "Think strong. Hang in there."

She began to experience daily headaches and frequent bouts with upset stomach, diarrhea, queasiness and strange floating sensations. Health problems were new to Kay,

"You are experiencing symptoms only," Glenda pointed out. "The stress has to be alleviated soon or you'll become very ill."

She also began to have trouble sleeping. She was wide awake anyway, so she used the wee hours to transcribe recorded notes into her journal.

When she could sleep, there were nightmares. In many Karl would suddenly appear. The dreams became increasingly more bizarre.

Kay had a puzzling premonition the morning after she and Glenda discussed filing a complaint against Karl. And she was spot on. About mid-morning he called and ordered her to his office.

She phoned Glenda. "He says he has a memo to discuss that is informational in nature about some problems and concerns he has with me. He said I could bring a union representative if I want. I don't know if I need the union or not."

"If he said *that,* you definitely need one," Glenda advised. "Were you aware you were under investigation?"

"No, not officially anyway. But I know I'm being watched."

"Policy says an employee must be officially notified by the supervisor if an investigation is underway," she continued. "Regulations also state that a supervisor must document several counseling sessions in which he tries to work out problems with the employee."

"Counseling sessions?" They both laughed.

The previous day, Karl had tried again to get Kay to initiate a sexual encounter in exchange for a good evaluation. When she returned from keying data, he appeared to be looking through his mail. They were essentially alone because the inmates had gone for the day and the teachers were busy in the learning center. First, he asked why it took so long to key the forms, so she figured he knew she and Glenda had talked.

Instead he said, "You are still not making me happy. If you don't start doing what I tell you and try to please me, I'll put you on written report."

He paused long enough to give her a chance to offer him something, but she walked around the desk, sat down and looked at him.

After a moment, he abruptly turned and spouted off as he went out the door, "I think I *will* write that report!"

Glenda surmised that since Kay did not fall for his tactics, he was following through with his threat.

"I'll try to talk to him first to see if we can work something out before we file on him. He needs to start acting like a decent supervisor," she said.

Kay wondered if she could file a sexual harassment complaint since he had not propositioned her in so many words. Instead, he tried to manipulate her into initiating an encounter.

"It doesn't matter how he does it," Glenda explained. "If a supervisor creates a hostile environment at the workplace, it's harassment under the law and you have the right file an EEO complaint against him. We can also claim 'harassment due to sex' because he's discriminating against you in every way conceivable because you're a woman. It's not only the sexual angle, it's everything combined. Besides, we know he has a history of this sort of thing."

Then Kay told Glenda something else that Dan had heard Karl say several times in conversations with other men, "I have no use for either women or niggers – my wife and daughters being the exception."

"The man is racist as well as a misogynist pervert," declared Glenda. "According to the union, all the women he had harassed at other prisons either dropped their complaints or were too intimidated to file on him."

"Well, I'm not afraid to," Kay declared. "I'll take it clear to the Supreme Court if I have to. He's got to be stopped before he ruins anybody else. He'll wish he'd never messed with me."

Lab Technician Susan Shultz accompanied Kay to Karl's office. Before they even shut the door, he demanded, "What's this woman doing here? I have nothing to say to her."

"She's my union representative."

Though obviously annoyed, Karl proceeded to hand them copies of an "Unsatisfactory Performance Memo" – the first step in the new progressive discipline process.

Kay's hands clenched two pages of blatant lies. Susan's eyes widened with shock as she read. Karl watched them from behind his large desk with a smug self-satisfied look on his face.

They listened for over an hour as he reiterated Kay's so-called inadequacies, not pausing long enough to give either of them a chance to get a word in edgewise.

"We might as well end this meeting," said Susan. "We're just bashing our heads against a stone wall."

In the hall, she emphatically stated, "That is *not* a nice man! I've never met anybody like *that* before in my life."

Kay's hands were still shaking ten minutes later when she handed the memo to Glenda.

After reading it, Glenda said, "I'm glad the Union's involved in this now, because I can't do much yet except give you moral support."

She continued that EEO counselors could not get involved in disciplinary matters except regarding the part they play in the actual harassment. But the material could be used for background information. Disciplinary cases are handled by the union.

"I'll begin the sexual harassment and discrimination report. If we can't work something out with Karl or the warden within a few days, we'll sock him with a complaint to the Bureau in DC."

They agreed that something had to be done and soon.

CHAPTER 5

THE BEAT GOES ON

Karl always suspended chewing-out sessions when someone else came on the scene only to resume when the person left. Sometimes he would leave the office when interrupted only to pick it back up the next time he had Kay cornered.

Karl came in earlier than usual one day, ignored Kay and headed straight for his mailbox. As he reached for the contents, he suddenly stopped, turned to her and said, "I *will* tell you every move to make! You've been allowed to do anything you want around here for too long."

About that time Dan came in, so Karl stopped in mid-sentence and began talking to the teacher in a pleasant tone. He picked up his mail as if nothing was going on, looked through it and started out.

From the door he tossed it toward Kay. It scattered over the papers she was grading. A couple of pieces slid onto the floor.

Dan picked up the spilled mail, laid them on her desk and handed her a memo he'd pulled from his mail slot.

It was from the warden notifying everyone that time sheets must be hand-carried by each supervisor to Human Resources every other Friday morning. No one was to keep his own time, so Dan had always kept Kay's. She was the timekeeper for the rest of the 20-member department.

Anxiety swept across her. Those sheets had to be in by 8:30 a.m. and Karl was never seen in the office that early. He was usually in the Safety Office having coffee, but Kay knew better than to call him or go there to find him.

On the next Friday, Karl surprised them by showing up at 8 a.m. sharp. Kay held the stack of long multi-copy forms toward him and said they were ready for his signature.

Without comment, eye contact or the least change of expression, he sat down at the mail table and quickly signed each one without even looking to see who it belonged to – until he came to Kay's. He finally signed it after studying each entry, then got up leaving the forms scattered where they were. Kay thanked him and said she'd have them separated so he could take them to HR.

Karl bristled, his look shooting through Kay like daggers. "I am *above* that, and I'm sure as hell *not* going to stand here and watch you tear them apart," he said.

On the next time-sheet day, the due time came and went with no sign of Karl. Kay began to panic but not only because of the time sheets. She had SAT tests scheduled to begin shortly. Someone had seen him coming in, so there was no alternative but to page him. He ignored it.

Kay knew there'd be a call soon from HR about the time sheets, so she called them. She could hear them discussing among themselves that Greiner refused to sign or deliver the time sheets. From the sound of the surprised voices, they found it difficult to believe that a supervisor was belligerently refusing to follow the warden's orders. Finally, they decided that under the circumstances the only thing to do was for Kay to find recreation supervisor Ben Byerly, have him sign the forms, then carry them up herself.

Less than five minutes after her return from HR, Karl sauntered into the office and without a word, went straight to his mail slot, took what was in it and left. He did not curse at her for paging him, but she had a feeling the proverbial would eventually hit the fan.

As she frantically tried to get the test started that was already almost thirty minutes behind schedule, Kay wondered how Karl could get away with such blatant disobedience.

"Like he said last time, he's too good for lowly work like signing time sheets. I bet he'd feel differently if *his* was among them," she thought.

Susan called to bring Kay up to date on the union's efforts to get Karl to remove the unsatisfactory memo from her personnel file.

"He wouldn't return my calls and when I finally did corner him, he told me he 'didn't have anything to discuss' with me," she said.

She said several union representatives had discussed the situation and decided that it might be better if a man handled Karl. He had been very rude to Susan. Maybe he would at least let a man in his office.

"Tom Hilton is probably the best person to take Greiner on, and he said he'd try to talk to him," continued Susan. "Tom's good people."

At first Kay couldn't believe anyone would want to help, but it didn't take long for her to realize that nearly everyone desired to give her both moral and emotional support.

Just as expected, Karl stormed into her office that afternoon and exploded. "Don't you *ever* page me on that intercom again! If I want to come over here, I'll come without your assistance. And don't you ever ask to have your lunch period moved again either. Your lunch hour being fifteen minutes late the other day disrupted the operation of the whole department."

No one in Education had ever had a set lunch time. They took 30 minutes at their discretion within the hour the department was closed. She had asked for the recent delay to keep a dental appointment.

"I have never dealt with an employee as worthless as you!" Karl yelled as he stomped out.

An hour later he was back. This time he said Kay had shown disrespect to a teacher (Earl, of course) by writing notes to herself *on her own work copy* of a list of new students.

"How on earth was *that* disrespectful? she asked.

"And you ate your lunch ten minutes late yesterday, too and were on the phone again!"

The previous day her so-called lunch break had been delayed by the delivery of sensitive supplies that could not be handled by inmates.

The only phone call she could think of that Karl had observed was a brief conversation with the vocational training teacher who had *called Kay* regarding new students to be added on computer. In addition, Karl had ordered that she make and receive all department phone calls. He made sure of that by having all other phone lines changed to the office number. They would discover part of the motive for the phone shuffle later.

Karl repeated his management training and how he had the right to tell Kay how and when to do everything in the office. "And that's not necessarily what's the most convenient for you."

He reiterated again that she did not manage time.

She wanted to say to him, "No longer than you stay around here each day – which is only long enough to either ignore or yell at me – how can you possibly know what I do."

By then they all knew that "Earl the snitch's" beady little eyes represented Karl's eerie presence. They wondered what Karl had promised him in return.

They would soon find out the extent of Earl's espionage.

Kay's sons were involved in activities which necessitated them being at school early almost every morning. After dropping them off, she would arrive at work thirty minutes before anyone else in the department. She cherished this uninterrupted time which was the only way she could accomplish anything. However, it would last only until Karl found out and put a stop to it. He had already forbidden her to stay late and would come around at the end of the workday to make sure she left. He did everything he could think of to keep her from getting any work done.

Union Representative Tom Hilton called after he tried to talk to Karl. "He just sat there like a robot and repeated your many, quote/unquote, "inadequacies" over and over, adamantly refused to budge. He absolutely will not remove that memo from your personnel file. I might as well have been talking to my old tom cat!"

A nice looking and well-built man in his late thirties, Tom was one of those unique individuals who could get along with anyone. Everybody liked him – line staff, middle management and administrators alike. Those qualities made him an excellent union steward – or union rep as they are called in the Bureau of Prisons. A military veteran and avid outdoorsman, he had much in common with most of the men and treated the female employees like ladies. In return, he was respected by all – even the inmates – as a fair and impartial correctional officer. His easy-going gift of gab was also entertaining as he described things in such a way as to paint word pictures. Tom was just plain fun.

He went on to say that the union officers had

discussed several possibilities such as invoking arbitration, an appeal to the Unfair Labor Relations Board or perhaps even going public. Sometimes tipping off the media about a problem could fix it pronto, but the warden's assistant was the only person authorized to release information to the public. Tom continued that the best thing to do in a case like Kay's was to write an anonymous letter to the editor. Problem with that is letters must have an author's authorized signature to be printed.

One day in exasperation, Kay asked Karl if she ever did *anything* right.

"That isn't the issue," he said without hesitation, "just what you're doing – not managing time well. It doesn't matter to me if anyone else lives or dies, I'll keep right on just like I have been."

She knew he would have too, because he sure did not give a rip about anybody else, especially her. A person like that does not even like himself, she thought.

"And I *will* tell you every move to make," he adamantly added.

That was when he assigned her the time-consuming and constant interruption of entering arrival and departure times on all inmate passes. Every morning, then again before and after noon as well as at count time 3:45 pm there were at least 100 inmate students. Add all education workers on call-out plus all library and law library traffic, a steady stream in and out.

Not only that, he changed her lunch time again, 11:45 to 12:15. They reopened at noon, so she had 15 minutes to eat. Not even enough time to walk to the employees' lounge.

"And you're not to vary from it one minute." To her plea for just a few minutes' leeway for unexpected events, he snapped, "No. Because I decided, that's why."

If Kay made the slightest attempt to explain something or ask a question, Karl considered it argumentative and belligerent. She felt completely hopeless, lost in a maze.

She had tried her best to do her job to his satisfaction but from the start, she felt damned either way. Responsibilities, quantity or quality of her performance were not considered.

"How I wish we had the big Dutchman back," she said to herself.

CHAPTER 6

KAY SPEAKS UP

It was obvious by then that Karl's ultimate plan was to get Kay fired – or worse. But how could the situation get any worse?

There was no way she could have understood the overall scope of Karl's plans. But when another supervisor told Tom something Karl was overheard saying, more of his nature was revealed.

"He swore he would beat you down until you either submitted to him or he got you fired – whichever came first," Tom said. "He referred to you as 'that suborn little bitch' and added he was not in the habit of letting a 'damn broad' hold out on him and get away with it.

"It's become a personal vendetta to him," Tom added.

Kay always scheduled a week off immediately after the school year ended to organize her household and the boys for the summer. To make sure her duties were covered, she asked Karl who would be giving the ABE tests while she was off so she could get supplies to him.

"I don't see that's any of your goddamned business!" he said as he glared down his nose.

Much to her relief, Dan later said he'd be administering the test while she was on vacation and asked about testing and grading materials.

The next week was heavenly, but it seemed over almost before it had begun. Out of sight was not out of mind. She had tried to focus on pleasant things, but Karl's image hung over her.

She felt sick as she dressed for work the next Monday morning. "I'd give anything in the world if I didn't have to go out there today," she said to her husband.

Not knowing what was going on at work he dismissed her comment as wishful thinking since everyone else in the family would be at home that day. He knew she was wound as tight as a banjo string. She still couldn't talk with him about her situation for fear of condemnation.

"Glad you're back," greeted Dan as she walked in. "Sure missed you and I bet you thought about us every minute too."

That statement made in jest was so close to the truth. Karl and Earl had been in her thoughts constantly but not by choice. The week off helped slightly but did not alleviate the effects from stress that were becoming obvious to Kay as well as to everyone else.

Kay did not see Karl early that morning but knew it was too good to last. About 10 a.m. the dreaded call came. He ordered her to his office "to go over something." She did not want to see him at all, especially not alone.

The usual knots formed in her stomach as she crossed hall and opened his door. He sat with papers fanned out on the desk in front of him. He handed her several loose pages and motioned toward a chair.

One paper was a daily minute-by-minute itinerary done by Earl while she was on leave. It listed her duties with firm beginning and ending times for each. He also had her doing several things at the same time such as filing, computer entries, opening and sorting mail.

Virtually and humanly impossible. Only 20 minutes had been allotted for one daily computer entry job that always took at least an hour. She tried to explain the time frames were unrealistic and that nothing she did was that absolute. In response, a hard-icy stare. Then he said, "Earl sat at your desk and did this schedule, so you do it. You follow it to the letter and if you don't, you'll be put on official report."

That list was obviously *all* he did in the office while Kay was gone because none of her work, except for Dan giving tests, had been touched. Nothing. He could not possibly have worked that schedule, because he had no way of knowing how long each of her daily tasks took. He had made it all up.

Kay knew that saying anything to Karl about any of the above would have brought more of his wrath down on her. All she wanted to do was to get out of his office.

She was thankful to Dan for doing the testing though. She'd have all the rest to catch up.

The first day back she found her radio missing. She finally located it in a bottom file cabinet drawer. Along with it were personal items like her coffee mug, hand lotion and a small cosmetics case. On top of the heap was her family photo and a bud vase, a secretary's day gift from Jim Datema and the others.

An inmate assigned to the print shop came in about the time she was placing her things back where they belonged.

He volunteered, "While you were gone, Mr. Norman was grippin' and cussin' just grabbin' those things and throwin' 'em in that drawer. When I asked him what he was doin' he said 'gettin' rid of her stupid stuff.' He had no right to get in your desk while you were gone and mess with your things."

She assured him that nothing was broken and that his concern was appreciated.

In her mind's eye, she could see Earl throwing his fit but could make no sense out of his childish behavior. Earl was very self-centered and wanted to suck up so bad. He would do about anything to get ahead including Karl's dirty work and would step on anyone to climb the career ladder. But it takes a very small person to do something that petty.

"That was just plain mean," she said aloud. "I wonder if he dumped my things to hurt me or, in his warped reasoning, an attempt to impress Karl. The payoff must be pretty big."

After lunch as Kay was constructing files for the prisoners admitted while she was on leave, Karl made his first appearance of the day. He stood in the door and looked around. Then as if he could not think of anything else, pushed her "out" basket toward the middle of the desk.

"Get this damned box off your desk right *now!* From now on you will use one of those mail slots over there. And get that 'franked' mail into one of those too!" he barked as he motioned toward the bank of small spaces along the wall.

He seemed to anticipate an objection. "I gave you an order! I'll run this office *my* way and that's not necessarily what's convenient for you."

The apparent present thrust was to rid her office of any hint of comfort or convenience. It was the second time in a week he had brought it up.

The next day she had to laugh out loud at all the mail crammed into the 3-inch slots. All the teachers – except Earl – were having a blast capitalizing on the situation. Mail spaces for "out-going" were jammed full, larger envelopes were crammed in, others were hanging out. One letter was clipped onto the corner of another that barely fit. Dan put paper clips and a large scotch tape dispenser on the table "just in case."

Karl totally ignored the entire display. Although ridiculous, it was hilarious. But as Dan said, "We might as well laugh about it, or we'll go crazy."

Kay's sense of humor was still intact, and she had the support of the other employees which was all that was saving her sanity. When faced with a situation this absurd most people would have lost it or given up. She had always had a strong constitution but had taken about all she could.

It became more difficult each day – no, impossible – to accomplish much of anything.

Each morning Kay wondered as she drove to work, "What will it be today? What else can he possibly come up with? He must lay awake nights dreaming up stuff. Who ever heard of an office where 'in' and 'out' boxes aren't allowed?

"Hindsight is so clear," she continued, "There is no way he'll ever accept me especially after he realized I would never submit to him sexually. It's my first experience with such an evil person. We aren't even wired the same way. I can't deal with him on his level."

At the same time Karl had ordered the desk trays removed, he stated, "'We' still have an issue to resolve, and 'we' will discuss it in my office in five minutes."

Kay figured he would again try to scare her into propositioning him or it would be another two-hour chewing out session.

She called Tom.

"Go on in and see what he wants, but don't accept or sign anything unless you're allowed union representation," was his advice.

Kay wanted to secretly record Karl to catch one of his tirades. Tom laughed and said he'd like nothing better but if the recorder made a noise to tip him off that he was being recorded without his knowledge, we could possibly lose the case if it ever goes to court. As it seemed to be headed in that direction they decided to stay on the safe side.

How she dreaded going over there. It took a few minutes to muster up the courage to cross the hall and face Karl.

The "issue" was unbelievable. This time Karl had accused her of breaching security and proposed she get an official letter of reprimand – the next step after the unacceptable performance memo. Before she even got to the part where he stated the false charges, she stopped reading, looked straight at him and blurted out, "You never quit, do you?"

He sat reared back in his large executive chair with his arms folded, staring at her, gloating with arrogant self-satisfaction. He was enjoying himself.

"Why are you doing this to me," Kay asked. "You really don't like me at all, do you? Do I remind you of someone or is it because I'm a woman?"

The word *woman* hit square on a raw nerve. He puffed up and exploded, "I don't dislike you; I don't even *know* you. And it's not because you're female or because you're black, white, Hispanic, Jewish, Protestant, Catholic…" and on and on and on…

He had memorized the discrimination policy.

"I can't understand why you criticize me for things my previous bosses commended me for."

He picked it back up in a mocking disgusted tone, "Yeah, I went up to HR and read your past excellent evaluations. *He* gave you *'exceeds'* last time! He should've looked at you closer."

She was so upset by then her eyes would not focus. According to his proposal she had violated institution security by simply getting up from the computer to unlock a door about six feet away. Nothing in that proposal was true. There was no inmate in her office. She did not violate policy.

"Do you want to discuss the memo further?" he taunted.

"Discuss? No, I do not."

"Well, just sign the bottom of it then," he ordered.

She was firm, "I will not accept this lie or sign this paper either without union representation."

"You don't need the damn union. If you don't sign that you got it, I'll just sign for you and state that you refused to sign. I'm *not* going to talk about it with you or the union, *now or ever!"*

She stood her ground. "I will not sign off on a complete falsehood and you can do whatever you want to!"

She turned and left his office.

Tom said what happened was unbelievable. He said to go ahead and sign when Karl asked again and assured her that he *would* ask again. He went on to explain that putting her signature on the memo was not an admission of guilt, only that she *received* the proposal. And the union needed a copy as soon as possible so they could get to work on it.

"He's enjoying every minute of this," he added.

They agreed the newest episode with the desk trays had been staged to give her one last chance to redeem herself. In other words, offer him something that would *please* him.

It came the next day when Karl demanded she come to his office to have a "friendly conversation" about the proposal. Instead, he raked her over the coals for two full hours.

First, he threatened, "I'm warning you not to try to transfer out of Education. If you put in for a job in another department, I'll have to tell that department head you are not a commendable or cooperative employee. You are argumentative, don't follow orders or try to please your supervisor and you do not manage your time well.

"Your job grade level is weak and if HR ever even thinks about raising it like the regional office said, I'll have to recommend against you no matter what they said on that desk audit.

"No one leaves this department unless I say so, and that goes for staff as well as inmates."

Jim had twice asked for a desk audit of her position during his futile attempts to raise the position grade to at least equal all other federal prisons. He based his request on the level of responsibility and her performance evaluations. The Regional Office had established the higher grade several years previously and subsequently established a statement to raise the grade of Kay's position accordingly.

The next day Tom brought his lunch over to discuss their defense. He would try to set up an informal meeting with Karl, the first step in fighting the charges. They had to stop talking several times because Earl kept coming in on some pretense or another to eavesdrop. He *had* to pull a file, check his mailbox, borrow a stapler, shred something…

The informal meeting with Karl was a total waste of time – cut and dried as was the formal one with the warden a week later. She received the official letter of reprimand.

Tom said the union would vote to appeal the warden's decision at their next meeting.

He then asked, "Did you know that the warden, Greiner, the safety officer and a whole bunch of 'em started out with the Bureau together?"

The *good 'ol boy* network was very strong at the medical center. It seemed strange that so many of them working there at the same time were about to retire. Some had been overheard bragging about transferring to a department head position near their desired retirement location just beforehand so the government would have to pay for their last move.

That explained a few things to Kay. Middle management and line staff had no chance against them. They no doubt owed each other plenty and probably had enough on one another to write a book. Karl was calling in a few markers.

Before the dust could settle on the letter of reprimand, he came into Kay's office grinning with anticipation. "I want you in my office in five minutes to go over something."

That sick feeling in her stomach returned. "Here we go again."

CHAPTER 7

OH NO! NOT AGAIN

Karl had given Kay five minutes to report to his office.

Tom's day ended at three and the thought of facing that tyrant alone terrified Kay. In about four minutes the phone rang. "I gave you five minutes to get over here!"

She started to explain she was trying to reach her union rep.

He interrupted loudly, "You don't need the damn union!"

She had to hold the phone away from her ear.

"This is a disagreement among staff! Get your ass over here right now!"

Karl was not the first person she saw as the door opened.

Reared back in the most comfortable chair, legs crossed and a smug look on his face, was none other than Earl.

Kay hesitated in the doorway.

"Get in here," Karl demanded.

She stepped in but remained by the partly open door repeating she wanted a union rep present.

"There's not going to be a union rep," he continued. "Shut the door and sit down!"

She inched onto the chair nearest the door. He handed her a two-page memo. Subject: Problems with Kay Richards. Considering everything else that had happened recently, nothing would be a surprise.

It was a ridiculous and childish document. Earl was reporting to Karl that she had accused him of eavesdropping on her phone conversations. Her mouth must have dropped in disbelief because Karl had a very self-satisfied look on his face.

"Staff came to me and told me you falsely accused Earl of eavesdropping," he said.

"What staff? Earl there?" she asked.

Karl did not reply so she addressed Earl directly. His facial expression remained frozen. He would not make eye contact but stared at the wall behind Karl's head.

"What do you mean 'falsely'?" she asked. "I wasn't the only one who saw you hiding back there on the floor in the corner of the learning center listening in on the only line. Two other people in my office also saw you."

Earl had been caught red handed. Kay had been talking to Tom that day when a girl from another department came to see her at lunch time. She saw

Earl, waved and said. "You're both on the phone."

Kay stood up and observed Earl hunched down in the corner, listening in to Tom and Kay discuss their defense of Karl's latest charges. He had stayed in when everyone else left for lunch.

The entire scene had also been witnessed by Ben who was checking his mailbox.

There had always been a straight phone line into the office as most calls went there anyway. Kay thought it asinine to hook all classroom phones to the office line. Made no sense whatsoever. She had picked it up a few times when someone was on it but always immediately hung up.

Kay originally chalked it up to one more obstacle to hurdle. But now another – or the real motive – was to allow Earl to spy on her. It also made sure the phone was not private, just like the fishbowl he had moved the office into. No wonder they always knew what she and the union were planning.

Back to the memo. As Kay read the last of it, she firmly said to Karl, "There's only one true statement in here. I did call him a snitch, because he is one!"

When Karl realized there were staff witnesses to the incident who would come to her defense, he said, "Give me back that memo. I'll tear it up."

Kay asked to make a copy first.

"You don't need a copy if I tear it up. Give it to me now."

"It says there's a copy in my personnel file."

"It's not gone up yet. I'll not send it if I tear it up."

They probably could not have forced Kay to

hand it over, but she felt outnumbered and stress effects a person's judgement. Reluctantly, she gave the memo back to Karl, but the photographic image of it remained etched in her mind. Tom said he would watch for a copy to mysteriously appear in her HR file.

Even before she left his office, Karl had a backup. He verbally accused her of "playing favorites" in the print shop. This is something she had been very careful not to do and had never even been accused of. Printing orders were always done on a "first come, first served' basis.

She reminded him that per his recent orders, nothing could be printed without his initials which always took several days. He did not speak further so she got up and walked out.

It was past time to go home and Karl was expected to pop in at any moment and order her to leave. She sat down at her desk and with tear-filled eyes, wrote from memory everything contained in Earl's hateful memo.

The day after he accused Kay of favoritism, Karl ordered the inmates to stop what they were doing and print tickets for the warden's going-away banquet. He even stood and waited for them. One of the "good ol' boys" was leaving and the higher up the transferee, the more lavish the affair.

To cover themselves, the inmates went to Kay immediately and reported what Karl had made them do. They knew that using supplies purchased with taxpayers' money to print personal material in a government print shop is illegal and a violation of institution policy.

A day or two later, while Kay ate lunch, she was writing on a birthday card for her brother when Ben came in followed a few seconds later by Karl. Karl spoke pleasantly to Ben but ignored Kay. While Ben pulled out his mail, Karl leaned against the door as if waiting to check his own mailbox.

Suddenly, like a switch was turned on, he addressed Kay. "What do you mean writing a note on that birthday card with a government pen during your lunch hour?"

Karl was blocking his way, so Ben stood there as Karl continued. "You are violating policy and it had better stop! Just let me remind you that you are the lowest graded person around here and you are to take orders from everyone else in this department."

He raised his voice accenting each word. *"Is that clear?"* He turned and went out the door. (The personnel chart showed the administrative assistant directly under the supervisor, the same as everyone else in the department.)

When the door closed Kay shook her head in pure exasperation as Ben said, "There goes a real piece of work."

Along about then Kay realized that Karl was either playing psychological games geared specifically to totally confuse her or he was completely crazy, probably both. They already had proof that his goal was to make her either quit or get fired.

She did not feel confused at that moment. She was mad.

"It's beyond me how the Bureau could keep a 'woman hater' like him. They either didn't see what he was up to or they just plain did not care," she said to Ben.

"He's definitely got a big daddy somewhere high up," Ben said.

"I know, but sexual harassment is against the law," she said, "and we have proof he's been disciplined, downgraded and transferred at least three times at other prisons before he came here."

Tom, Glenda and Kay discussed the overall situation many times. If Kay was fired due to trumped up charges or forced to quit because of stress related illness brought on by the intense harassment, she could have had reduced or possibly canceled retirement benefits. She was her family's main breadwinner and insurance carrier since her husband broke his back in an accident. With six sons to raise, she had to keep on working no matter what. She just *had* to.

One day when she saw Karl coming into the office, she just could not resist. She reached into her purse and pushed the record button on her small recorder.

After work in the parking lot Tom was smiling as he held the recorder to his ear. Don Douglas walked by and grinned. He shook his head and said, "I don't even want to know."

It was a blast getting Karl on tape, but they agreed to keep it private.

There was no telling of what this man was capable. Karl's most blatant disrespect, inexcusable behavior and insensitive indifference to Kay as a human being was yet to be demonstrated.

Karl took off almost every Friday for a three-day

weekend leaving Ben as acting supervisor. Fifteen minutes before time to go home on one of those days, Kay returned from keying data to find Ben in the office with another supervisor who was using the copy machine.

Dan rushed in with an urgent look on his face, "Kay, the county sheriff just called. I tried to catch you at Glenda's. You're supposed to meet the ambulance at the hospital!"

A terrible chill ran through her as he continued, "Your husband's been in an accident... Got his arm in a chain saw. They're on their way right now."

Dan verified with Ben that Kay wouldn't be charged leave for only a quarter hour under these circumstances and as she rushed out, Ben said to let them know.

Kay's husband and a friend had been cutting fireplace wood. A limb fell from a tree and knocked him onto the saw which was still running. His right arm was nearly severed just above the wrist. After six hours in surgery, the doctor gave him little hope of ever regaining full use of his hand.

Between the three men who were present when the emergency call came in and employees working that night, word got around to practically everyone at the prison about the accident. Ben called Kay at home the next day. He also included the incident in his duty officer report to Karl.

On Monday everyone she met asked about her husband. Everyone, that is, except Karl and Earl. Not a word. They totally ignored the entire incident.

First thing that morning, though, Karl went straight to Dan and ordered, "Charge her fifteen minutes annual leave for last Friday."

Dan had not entered leave for that time since Ben had approved, but Karl waited and watched Dan mark it down. They were already convinced Karl was a first-class heel, but this confirmed it.

Ben shook his head when he heard and said no one else would even think of doing such a thing. Besides, Kay was thirty minutes early almost every morning.

Ben paused as he reached into his mailbox, then turned toward Kay and said, "Another thing I can't figure out is why he placed so much emphasis on me 'watching you' while I was acting supervisor."

Karl had theoretically "slapped Ben in the face" when he undermined the authority he had given Ben when appointing him acting.

Two days later Kay needed time at the end of the day to take her husband to have the bandages changed. She would rather have taken a beating than approach Karl for permission to leave early.

"What's he going to do when you get him anyway? He can just wait a few minutes longer," was the uncaring answer.

When she asked him to reconsider, he sat down on the corner of his desk, his eyes fixed on her chest and leaned toward her. The corners of his mouth turned up slightly.

"Look, you cooperate with me and I'll think about doing you a favor or two."

She remembered then that the department was closed for the evening, so she backed toward the door and opened it.

He realized she would not be coerced so he stood

and stated, "Your being by yourself doesn't concern me. That's what you're supposed to be, you..." He caught himself, paused, then continued. "I'll take your damn job away from you a bit at a time and that includes that stupid print shop if you can't stay here and watch what goes on in it."

At 3:30 pm on Friday two days later, Karl came into her office and said flatly, "I need about five minutes of your time to go over something in my office."

This time he was alone when she went in. Without even asking her to sit down, he grinned and said he had a proposal for her to read.

She wanted to call Tom.

"You don't need a stupid damn union rep because all I'm doing is handing you this proposal."

A nervous wreck anyway, she nearly went to pieces when she saw what it said. This time he had falsely accused her of two more security violations and set the suspension at 14 days, the next step in the discipline policy.

He then said, "I hate doing this. I really do. I hate it."

"Yeah, right," she said, and without another word, she took the folder and left his office. She had never come so close to losing it as she did right then.

It was good the inmates were gone. Dan was alone. Stunned, she sat by his desk and tried to tell him what had just happened. Visibly shaken and trembling, she could hardly speak.

In his usual sympathetic fatherly manner, he said she should stay there with him as long as she wanted.

Karl had picked the worst possible time to give her that proposal – just before 4 on Friday afternoon – to ruin her weekend. Never missed a trick.

Tom and Glenda usually left at three, but Dan handed Kay the phone and urged her to try Glenda's office anyway. She was trembling so bad she could hardly dial the three-digit number.

Glenda picked up after only one ring. She said to come over there as soon as possible.

"Go right now," Dan said. "I'll ward him off if he comes in here looking for you."

Glenda said she had never seen Kay so shook up and added, "That jerk is making you sick."

She still had not been able to corral Karl long enough to discuss the EEO complaint. "He's almost never in his office and when he does answer the phone, he has no time for me. Won't make an appointment either, avoids me like the plague."

Kay was ready to give up. "We'll never work anything out... never, ever... I just want to stay as far away from him as possible."

Glenda tried to cheer her up by reminding her of how Tom always says when he's low that if he looks up, he sees a snake go by.

Kay could not help smiling. Glenda continued to be upbeat explaining that Tom and the union would fight the unfair discipline charges. All that information could also be used in her EEO claim because the men in the department were not treated the same way. They were never disciplined, even when they needed it. This proved that Karl was discriminating against her because she's female.

This was in addition to his unwanted advances were clearly sexual harassment.

Glenda's EEO supervisor in the central office had stated they had a strong case. She knew Karl from a previous station said Karl's reputation had spread throughout the Bureau, then asked if he had changed.

Glenda answered with an emphatic, "No, he hasn't. And he's messin' with Kay now and no one in the front office will do a thing about it."

CHAPTER 8

THE FISH BOWL

K ay's life had become more out-of-kilter every day since Karl arrived at the prison. He and his newest proposal haunted her throughout the weekend, and it was clear the strain was affecting her life at home.

"Mom! All I said was 'I'm hungry' and you yelled at me," her youngest told her after one tense incident.

She hadn't said anything to the kids about Karl except that he was cranky, but her oldest also sensed something was wrong. "I think your new boss is making you nervous," he said. "You ought to get away from him."

She knew he was right, but what could she do? She had years of experience, but only a two-year associate degree. There were few positions at her grade or higher that didn't require mobility and at least a four-year degree.

The next week Karl came into the office stomping and kicking electric cords on the floor out of his way. Per his earlier orders, electric outlets were across the room from all the machines.

"I haven't seen a work order to get rid of these damn cords," he raged.

She reminded him that he refused to sign her request. He then gave her a blank stare and walked out. She did another work order immediately to either move the outlets or install new ones.

Not only did Karl refuse to sign that work order too, he exploded. "You expect me to ask a crew over here and cost the taxpayers $30 or $40 to put outlets in just for your convenience? It's my money too, and I don't want to see it wasted. And you don't need that clock!"

The clock was necessary to time SATs not to mention trying to follow Earl's senseless schedule. Besides, it was irrelevant. The clock was plugged in across the room in one of the original outlets. Ironic he would bring up taxpayers' money so soon after he spent several thousand tax dollars on new furniture for his own rarely occupied office.

It was inconceivable the bureau would condone his crazy behavior. He had to have friends and/or influence in high places. Taking this into consideration, Dan warned her to be extremely careful from now on because it looked like they'd pulled out all the stops.

Karl had moved the office into the least desirable

location in the entire area, part of his campaign to harass her, and put her in the most unsafe and inconvenient place.

Also, the dreariest. Karl had overheard a comment Kay made about how plants in the office window brought the outdoors in. He seemed to be ignoring her as usual but apparently had filed it away for the future. Kay had always loved nature and the outdoors. Being stuck back in that hole with no access or view to the outside was depressing. She was not claustrophobic, but it made her nervous for safety reasons. There was only one way out, and the door could *not* be locked from inside.

Two walls were of single-pane unreinforced glass from about three feet up which made the room look like a fishbowl stuck in the mouth of a cave. About 10 feet square, probably a fourth the size of her last office, there was barely enough room to walk between furniture and equipment. The copier ended up in the classroom just outside the office door. One small yellow light fixture hung overhead and with no window, the room really did look like a cavern. With no air circulation, it was stuffy and smelled musty.

The location, in the busiest place in the department, made no sense. Before the move, Kay could supervise the print shop through a large glass window. The office was also spacious and private. Afterwards, she had to lock up and go down the hall to check on how, or if, work was progressing. To make the move even more asinine, her old office was left vacant.

For the first time Kay became concerned about

her safety. Correctional employees accept the fact that an element of danger is always present, but part of the job and kept in the background.

The only fire escape was through three classrooms. If an assaultive inmate came around the desk at her, she'd have to go over the top of the desk to evade him. If she had time the phone could be knocked into the narrow crevice between the desk and wall. An attacker could not retrieve it before the automatic alarm system went off.

A young first-time offender told Kay that many inmates were concerned that she was the only woman they had seen in the institution who did not wear a body alarm.

Karl answered Kay's request for one with, "The captain's office doesn't have any extra body alarms right now." That was the last she ever heard about it.

According to Tom, a policy had been in effect for years requiring any person working around inmates to wear a body alarm, but it was not enforced.

During the few weeks he had worked in the print shop, the young inmate gave Kay several memos describing different situations he witnessed. He then put himself on the firing line when he said to Karl that they "shouldn't be so mean to Ms. Richards."

"Let me tell you something, boy," Karl bellowed. "If you ever come between staff again, you're canned!"

It was difficult to keep the computer screens hidden from inmates' view due to limited space and glass walls. Two days after Kay had finally determined the best way to pack everything in, Karl ordered it all moved per his own arrangement plan. Again, she had only two outlets.

And Karl again was cursing the extension cords necessitated by his own refusal to approve enough electric outlets.

The most recent cord episode happened just before Kay began administering a scheduled SAT. She was surprised when immediately after the test started, a sheet metal foreman and his inmate crew showed up with Karl. They had come to install a pass-through opening in the wall between the office and hall. Karl declared that Kay would now sign the hundreds of inmate passes in and out each day. In addition, there would be constant inquiries plus the noise from the corridor would seem even louder.

She asked the foreman if a shelf could be built just under the opening.

"Forget it," Karl interrupted. "Don't need that!"

"Keep out of this, Karl," said the foreman. "If she wants a shelf, we'll make her a shelf!"

Karl shut up and left.

Kay thanked the foreman for speaking up for her, and he apologized for working during school hours. His supervisor was one of Karl's drinking buddies, he said, and Karl had come to mechanical services early that morning and demanded the job be done that very day.

"We had several jobs planned today; a week's work ahead of him; he didn't even have a work order," he added.

The test was given to the broken rhythms of jig sawing, hammers pounding, sheet metal rumbling, shop carts rattling, tools dropping and workers hollering as they trooped back and forth through the classroom, the only way into the office.

In addition, Karl allowed a law library clerk to come into the classroom and run the copier for thirty minutes. The inmate had said he didn't mind waiting for a break in the test to make the routine copies, but Earl told Karl that Kay had made the inmate wait.

Karl went straight into the classroom and told the inmate to proceed: "It doesn't matter what she says. I give the orders around here."

After Kay noticed a steady stream of inmates going through to the learning center and another classroom, she discovered that Earl had purposely locked the hall entry doors to both rooms. This forced the student traffic through where twenty men were trying to take a test.

Karl had refused her request to postpone the exam until the work crew had finished or move the group to another area. By late morning she was exhausted, exasperated, hoarse and her throat hurt.

The inmates complained about the conditions for the test which could not be retaken. They had good reason to claim their scores were affected.

At lunch time, Dan offered to sit in the room with two men who were not finished with an untimed portion of the test so Kay could go for the mail. She had already risked Karl's wrath by not going on the mail run at the exact time listed on her so-called schedule.

That afternoon Karl wanted to know why she left two inmates testing without supervision. When Kay replied Dan was with them, Karl declared, "I'm going to ask Williams about it and if he doesn't back up your story, I'll want a memo.

"That's ridiculous," Dan said. "We leave students in each other's care all the time."

The next morning, Karl played one of his little games with Dan.

He told Dan he was going to recommend a bump in his grade level and then quickly asked him if Kay had left two inmates by themselves taking the test on Friday.

Dan confirmed he was with them, and that Earl was also there. Then Karl asked if he was sure he didn't want to change his mind about it. Dan stated he couldn't change the facts.

"That has to be the lowest… trying to bribe me to lie in exchange for a promotion," Dan said later.

Dan then assured Kay that he would back her till the end even if Karl turned into the "best man on earth tomorrow."

He was close to retirement and didn't care what the "higher ups" did to him. He was not the least bit afraid of them and they knew it. With his heart condition he could retire on a "medical" at any time but wanted to stay long enough to be eligible for full retirement. He was sure they would not mess with him so late in the game.

Kay really did not know what she would have done without Dan. A stable force in her life right then, he was the only one in the department she could completely trust.

CHAPTER 9

JURIS KANGAROO

How much more would Karl get away with before someone higher up stepped in. It was one incident after another with no apparent interference from administration.

One unbelievable series of events began mid-morning when Karl burst into Kay's office. "Move everything out into that classroom," he ordered. "I'm putting carpet in here."

The tiny room was already so full of furniture the floor was hardly visible. Ridiculous, but Kay knew better than to question him.

"The installation crew will be here at one, and you'd better have it all out by then," he barked.

Kay carried her current work into the classroom. Inmates took the desk and other large pieces apart so they would go through the door. They were ready with fifteen minutes to spare so she sent the prisoners back to their jobs and sat down at part of her desk to do time sheets.

About 1:30, Karl came cruising in. Upon hearing the carpet crew had not been seen or heard from, he picked up the phone and appeared to be inquiring. "Is that right? Well... The 20th? OK."

He hung up and turned to Kay, "Put all this stuff back. They're coming Thursday at 1 o'clock."

Kay said they could operate out of the classroom the next two days, but...

"I said, put it all back in," he interrupted angrily.

Too frustrated by such nonsense to even think, she sat dejected, staring at the door he had just exited.

The inmates were confused too. They joked that they'd make as much money moving it back as they got moving it out, but one middle-aged man from Colombia was puzzled. "Move...desk...back in?" he asked in broken English.

"Carpet day" began as organized chaos. Karl came by early to order the office be cleared out again and then made another brief appearance after lunch to make sure the place was stripped.

Kay was alone in the learning center with Earl because Dan had a medical appointment in the afternoon. The press was down so the print shop was locked, and those inmates were working in another classroom.

But a carpet crew arrived right on schedule and was finished in no time.

That was when Earl left, leaving Kay alone with

more than 100 inmates

She had no body alarm and there were no officers or other employees nearby in the building. There were more than eighty student inmates and twenty more in the afternoon computer class. Inmate clerks and classroom workers stream in and out of the libraries. It was impossible for one person to effectively supervise that much space and that many prisoners.

Earl had left her in a precarious position.

She had often been left alone but had never felt in danger. She had always taken the prescribed precautions anyway to be on the safe side, memorizing numbers for the nearest officer posts and staying in position to set off an alarm just in case. She was not uneasy or afraid but disgusted.

With the furniture still not replaced on the carpet, she backed herself against a wall in the office where she could observe most of the area through the glass,

Dangerous as this may seem to an outside observer, she was safer in this environment than it would appear. Inmates rarely threaten female employees. On the contrary, they tend to be protective of them.

They like the atmosphere of having females in the institution – at least to look at – and the mere presence of women has a tranquilizing effect on male prisoners.

After Earl left, Kay kept hearing noises like nuts and bolts rattling. She tried not to be obvious trying to find the noise. It always came from the same place, but she could not locate it.

She had earlier overheard an education inmate worker brag, "Just give me enough time and I'll have this place cleaned out good." Other inmates snickered while giving her quick side glances.

Then she observed the "bragger" inmate trying to hide a long screwdriver in his pants as he went out the door.

Every prison employee, no matter what his or her position, is first a correctional officer. It was up to her alone to control this situation and do it quickly.

Following the inmate would violate security by leaving unsupervised inmates with expensive equipment and telephones.

Not acting on her observation would be "allowing an inmate access to a class A tool" which in this case could easily be made into a "shank."

She went to the door and watched him go down the hall and up the stairs, so she knew where he was headed. She went down the list of officers' numbers, finally reaching the timekeeper for the Corrections Department. He sent help and advised her to secure the area.

Meantime, the inmate who had taken the screwdriver came back, so he was also locked inside.

It had made no sense for this inmate to be assigned to an education work detail where most of the workers were white-collar – businessmen, teachers, lawyers and other educated individuals – people who could contribute in some way. Big and burly, he looked and acted like the renegade biker he had been before prison. Kay tried to convince herself that her bewilderment at his mere presence was only her imagination because she was aware of his past.

While Kay talked to the officer who came to help, inmates kept glancing their way and the biker seemed a bit uneasy.

Suddenly, Earl came back. He acted puzzled, as if he did not know what to do. Kay suggested they lock the door again and shake down the area.

"I guess that'll be all right," he mumbled.

It is not unusual in a prison for electrical equipment to disappear and turn up later minus motors that had been made into tattoo machines. Several recorders, players, fans and wall clocks had been taken from the department before everything was bolted down.

And a CD player turned up missing from the exact area where Kay kept hearing the noise.

Kay and the officer stood by the door checking each inmate before he was allowed to leave. But the biker inmate had not left with the others.

Kay suggested that Earl check the restroom, but he just stood there as if not knowing what to do or did not want to do it. The man was inside, but Earl did not pat him down which is at least minimal, so the officer did.

Earl hesitated a bit when Kay suggested he quickly shake down the rest room. Standing by the door the inmate fed Kay a "cock and bull" story about going to his locker to put away a can of machine oil and his own small screwdriver. He claimed that when he came back the other inmates "front streeted" him believing they would all get in trouble because of his actions. Earl then came out of the rest room, unlocked the door and just let him out.

About that time Dan came in from his medical appointment. Unlike Earl, he was interested in getting to the bottom of the missing player. He and Kay together shook down the resource center where the biker spent most of his time but found nothing else missing. They reasoned the player could have been concealed in the large man's loosely fitting pants when he left the first time with the long screwdriver. It was also possible that he had passed it through the bars of the bathroom window to someone outside in the yard or tossed out of sight on the ground to be picked up later.

About 3:45 Karl appeared and "very innocently" asked what was going on. Kay started to explain, but he abruptly cut her off and directly addressed Earl. "How did the inmate get that screwdriver?"

"I gave him one out of the print shop to fix a player," was the reply. The screwdriver had been removed from a secured tool cage in the locked room without signing it out.

Dan and Kay could hardly believe what they had just heard. Earl had just admitted that he gave an assaultive inmate what could have been a lethal weapon. He then left the area leaving Kay with all those prisoners. That's forbidden even if only one inmate was in the area.

Karl's facial expression had not changed since he came on the scene. To Kay, he said, "You do a memo," and then to Earl, "We'll discuss this in my office."

When they were alone, Kay asked Dan, "Why

are they discussing this? They weren't even here."

"Probably over there licking their wounds," was his reply. He then said directly to her, "Great detective work, Kay."

The large screwdriver that was missing from its place in the locked print shop tool cage was later hanging back where it belonged.

Kay wrote the memo Karl demanded but did not give it to him. It went straight to the investigative officer. Dan agreed, adding that was exactly what he would do.

A serious incident with the potential of developing into a very dangerous situation was averted. They never figured out what Karl and Earl hoped would happen, but one thing was for sure, it would not have been to Kay's good. Karl never asked her about that memo and neither of them ever mentioned the incident again.

Eagle-eye Earl stalked Kay's every move. Tom called it "houn' doggin'" but in any case, they had to be careful when using the office phone. He called Kay from home to make plans to meet with Glenda at lunch time a few days later to figure out how to handle the present charges.

When that day came, Tom carried chairs into Kay's office for himself and Glenda. He placed his in the narrow space between the desk and the door—blocking the entrance to prevent interruptions. The door would not lock from the inside.

Seeing them in the office together was about all Earl could stand. They were amused when he glared at them through the glass as he paced back and forth through the adjoining room. His attempts to open the door against Tom's chair were ignored. If he came close to the thin wall, they stopped talking or changed to an irrelevant subject. Tom suggested they could sing a school rally song.

Tom always referred to Dan's memo describing Earl and Karl discussing how to "get rid" of Kay as "the big gun." They agreed to keep it secret for a while because they knew the ammunition would be needed later. He felt they would have no trouble getting the current charges dismissed without it.

It was during this meeting that Tom realized Karl was lifting words for his disciplinary proposals verbatim out of the explanations in the memos he demanded from Kay after each trumped-up charge.

One of Karl's accusations was that Kay violated security by allowing the inmate in the room after he had ordered that no inmate was to set foot in the office. But he would have had no way of knowing that the inmate was there holding the printer together so it would function without getting that information from Kay's explanation.

Karl had demanded the non-sensitive document be typed immediately, but Kay needed the inmate's help to make the printer work. A "snitch" letter from Earl had said only that the prisoner was in the office. Not that it mattered, Karl found out why he was in there from Kay's own memo.

In another accusation Karl stated the exact test for which Kay was giving directions that she had also included in her memo.

"Next time he asks you for a memo, pretend you don't know what he's talking about," Tom said.

Pointing to one of the charges, Tom continued with a grin, "I see he didn't like it because you used the word 'mandated' in your memo. Apparently, the word struck a nerve."

It was amusing because that was exactly what he did – mandated that she use a busy open classroom as a testing site.

As he leaned his chair back against the door, Tom commented that someone should inform Karl that there is still freedom of speech in this country. They also discussed why Earl was not disciplined when he left his key unattended in the computer terminal for two hours as well as the screwdriver incident. Tom always heard through the union whenever someone was written up, and those had not been reported.

"Funny that Earl was never disciplined for negligence when the test answer sheets were stolen from a locked file on a weekend and sold among the inmates," Tom said.

As soon as he could get through the door, Earl huffed into the office. The scowl on his face must have only hinted at how mad he really was.

Kay had discovered Earl's key in the terminal one afternoon about 3:30. Prominently displayed on the screen was student information that could be read by looking through the glass. She called Dan for a witness, made a hard copy of the screen to document the time it was brought up, then turned off the computer and snapped his key on her key ring.

"He'll be back," Dan said with a grin, "and I can't wait to see the look on his face when he comes through that door."

Earl's absence since before 2:30 was not at all unusual as he had a bad habit of disappearing for long periods leaving students in class. He could not go home though without checking in that key. Four o'clock came and went.

Just as Dan was saying, "Shouldn't be too long now…" the door flew open and a very worried man rushed in.

White as a ghost, he said not a word, not even a glance in their direction. The look on his face clearly revealed his panic. He made a bee line for the terminal, then stopped abruptly, looked around and turned even more ashen. That was when Kay unhooked his key, held it up and jiggled it as she asked cheerily, "Is this what you're looking for?"

Reaching toward it, he mumbled sourly, "I guess you're going to tell *him*."

She handed it to him and said, "I'm not a rat. I don't enjoy getting other people in trouble."

He took the key and left; the scowl frozen on his tightly drawn face. Didn't even say "thanks."

Talk about making someone's day. Payback time, at least partially. The look on Earl's face when he rushed back to retrieve his key was epic. Clearly reflected was some of the misery he had helped inflict on Kay.

"He's definitely worried," Dan said with a grin when the door closed. "This was a real violation and he knows it. You have every right to report him."

"They would have just turned it around and accused me of criticizing a higher graded employee or something." Kay said.

She said nothing to Karl.

They knew Earl would never report himself. Tom and Glenda enjoyed the escapade as much as Dan and Kay did.

On Monday morning, Kay's radio could be heard from way down the hall, but the sound really blasted her when she opened the door. Nothing could have prepared her for what was inside.

The office had been trashed. Mail was on the floor, wastebaskets overturned and every single light in the place and all the machines were turned on. File drawers were unlocked and wide open and to make it personal, Kay's coffee mug, makeup kit and family photos were dumped into a trash can.

It had to be Earl.

Tom said, "He was as mad as a wet hen about being kept out of our meeting."

He was usually the first one out the door at the end of the workday, so the others noticed it was unusual that he had stayed when they left Friday. The department was always closed over the weekend.

Dan shook his head and said he was surprised that Earl had stooped that low. Tom summed it up by saying, "This sure shows the kind of warped personalities we're dealing with."

Glenda finally got an appointment with Karl and tried to discuss Kay's EEO complaint. He kept her in his office for over an hour relating, then reiterating, all of Kay's so-called inadequacies. She said later that he really got organized before he hit Kay with this one. He was using the Progressive Discipline Policy as a game plan and following it to the letter.

"He's the most unprofessional supervisor I've ever met," she added.

When they realized Karl was writing disciplinary proposals before he even asked for an explanation, then using Kay's words to insert charges. She remembered seeing the one he had started about the test laying on his desk the morning before he gave her the proposal.

It said, "On August 8, I observed...;" He even had the date wrong. The test was the next day."

Kay already swore she had written her last "explanation" memo. "Next time, I'll do just as Tom said – play dumb."

The next day the HR supervisor paid them a visit. Wayne Robbins had started out as a correctional officer a few years earlier and moved up through the ranks. He was thought to be too nice for that high-profile office with its potential to turn friends into enemies. On the other hand, everyone felt it better to have someone in the position who seemed to care.

Wayne handed Kay a short memo and said Karl had submitted more material to the last proposal, so her response time was extended two weeks. The additional documents included every single derogatory memo about Kay that Karl or Earl had written since their crusade began.

"This is called 'piling on' and it's pretty doggoned low," Tom emphasized, adding that none of it was even relevant to the case.

Another week passed before Tom was able to reach Karl by phone.

"Are you aware that Earl Norman left his key in the computer while he was away from the department for almost two hours?" he calmly asked as soon as he had an appointment.

The way Karl hummed, hawed and stammered clearly indicated he was surprised even though he claimed he already knew.

Tom continued, "This was witnessed by Dan Williams and Kay Richards."

With no mention of Dan, Karl asked, "Why didn't she report this to her supervisor and not to you?"

"She's not a snitch, that's why," Tom replied, followed by silence on the other end of the line.

"What kind of discipline did he get?" Tom continued. "You gave Kay a letter of reprimand for something a lot less severe."

"He got a verbal," was the curt response.

Tom knew there was no record of discipline in Earl's personnel file. Karl was squirming and Tom loved it. After a few seconds, Karl said dryly that policy did not require him to report insignificant counseling session with employees.

"You recorded false incidents about Kay though," Tom added.

Tom would have loved to push him further but thought it best to quit while ahead. He still had to deal with him regarding his ongoing vendetta against her. He said later that when he checked Kay's personnel file, he saw "garbage" that no other supervisor would have ever submitted.

This informal discipline meeting with Karl was exactly like the one after the letter of reprimand – a total waste of time. Like a broken record Karl repeated her "many inadequacies and imperfections" several times and then, with a closed mind, insisted the proposal stand.

Tom requested to meet with the new warden. Although disciplinary matters fall under the union, Glenda could attend as computer security officer but not as Kay's EEO counselor.

Warden Preston did not seem to be a part of Karl's clique. He was a classic picture of a trim clean-cut Marine Corps retiree and had a quiet pleasant demeanor unlike the traditional tough guy image of a prison warden. He had a reputation for being fair and seemed to already have a good rapport with staff and inmates.

Tom, Kay and Glenda felt that maybe he would at least be fair.

When the time came, Tom was prepared for battle, but Kay was nervous.

The warden read the charges against her regarding the inmate being in the office to hold the printer together and her not timing the SAT test which he pulled out of thin air – a total falsehood. Karl was asked if there was anything else he wanted to add or clarify.

"It's all in there. She's had performance problems ever since I got here," he said with finality.

It was difficult for Kay to sit quietly while he ridiculed everything about her as a person as well as her performance, not to mention the proposal which was a bold face lie. Tom had advised Kay not to say a word unless asked no matter how nasty Karl got, so she gritted her teeth and kept her eyes fixed on the large Department of Justice and Bureau of Prisons logos on the wall behind the warden.

Next Warden Preston listened intently as Tom brought out about the amount of time that elapsed between the alleged incident and request for a memo and about the date of the so-called offense being wrong. He emphasized that the printer was only printing what was on the screen and the inmate involved had been designated by Karl, himself, to duplicate and then distribute the same material. Every now and then the warden would ask a question to clarify a point.

He then asked Glenda to testify about the incident in relation to a security breach. She first described sensitive information in general terms, adding that no violation of security was committed simply by having the inmate hold the printer together so it would function.

When Warden Preston addressed Kay, she explained that the printer had been broken for less than a day, and a repairman was expected after noon. It would work only with the help of a second person. Karl had ordered no inmate was to set foot in the office, and staff people were not allowed to help Kay. He also ordered the copies be done immediately.

The repairman had said the printer appeared to have been sabotaged as he only needed to screw a couple of parts back together.

Then Tom addressed the second charge. He discussed the fact that the Program Statement referenced by Karl in the proposal letter did not mention time limits on testing. However, it did state that the test be given in a quiet area with no interruptions.

"Greiner is violating the same policy that he is falsely accusing Kay Richards of violating, because the testing site in which he demanded the test be given does not fit the criteria," Tom said.

Warden Preston then discussed the circumstances with Kay asking how the instructions were given to the inmates and what method was used to time the test.

Tom appeared to have the finesse of a court room lawyer as he summarized. He stated that conditions were met entitling Kay to union representation, but Karl had denied her that right. He then pointed out that the memos added later to the proposal did not pertain to the charges – in particular, the ones regarding Kay's work performance and moving the computer at another time.

When he concluded the warden complimented him, "You've certainly done your homework!"

Karl also falsely claimed he had counseled Kay on numerous occasions regarding each of the two charges. This simply was not true. He did, however, yell, curse, rant, rave, discriminate, verbally and emotionally abuse, insult, belittle, demean, degrade, snub, ignore, put down – in other words, harass.

On the way out, Tom said, "Neither Karl nor Earl refuted a thing we said."

Glenda added they got no support from the warden or Wayne either.

Kay expressed deep appreciation for their time

and efforts to which Tom stated, "If we didn't totally believe in you, we couldn't have done it."

After a few days, Wayne brought a draft of the hearing minutes. Kay noted several discrepancies in the transcript. A word left out or inserted can totally change the meaning, so she made a few changes and gave it to Tom for his input. He would get it back to Wayne so a final draft could be prepared.

Two days later, Tom saw Karl coming out of Wayne's office. After that, Wayne was in Karl's office for quite a while. Later in the day, Karl and Earl stayed in Karl's office for over two hours. Then Kay saw them start off toward the front end together carrying a thick folder.

Mid-afternoon Karl came into Kay's office wanting two more memos: (1) An explanation about a small note he claimed to have found on Kay's desk and (2) A roster that an inmate supposedly picked up from his office a few days ago. She thought perhaps he was starting early on his next case because he had heard that the warden was going to drop the last one.

"Don't write those memos," advised Tom. "If he presses you, call me and I'll try to talk to him."

About twenty minutes later her phone rang. "Come over here," demanded the threatening voice that hung up before she could reply.

Trembling she called Tom again.

"Go on in but if he wants to do anything more than hand you something, call me back."

Karl and Wayne were both there. Looked like trouble. Kay immediately asked to call her union rep.

Wayne spoke up, "All we're going to do is hand you the typed minutes of the last meeting and the final response from the warden."

Karl shoved a paper toward her to sign. She noticed and noted the warden's verdict had been rendered before Tom and Kay had even ok'd the final draft of the minutes.

They appeared to be hurrying Kay because Karl stated that all changes had been made, but she still insisted on reading it first. One important point had been omitted regarding Karl's claim he had counseled her. It must have been in the union's favor, because Karl resisted inserting the true facts.

Karl's look of anticipation caused her to expect the worst. She was not about to let him have the pleasure of seeing her reaction to the warden's decision, so she returned to her own office.

Kay's spirits lifted momentarily because the charge regarding the SAT test was completely dropped. As she read on, though, a knot as big as a football formed in her stomach. The warden had decided in Karl's favor on the charge she had violated security when the inmate touched the printer but gave no supporting reasons for his decision.

"Accordingly, you are to be suspended for one day," he wrote.

When she reached the parking lot after work, Tom was already leaning against his car. He said the union would file for arbitration within the week, then told her something he had learned that must be kept in strictest confidence. If word got back that the information was leaked to the union, someone could lose her job.

"The warden sees right through Karl and Earl and so does Wayne for that matter," Tom said. "Preston was going to drop both charges. In fact, he seemed to be agonizing over it. That's why he took so long deliberating."

Also, Karl and Earl have been in the warden's office with the door shut more than once, Tom continued. "Preston said he finally compromised and gave you one day administrative leave 'to get them off his back.'"

CHAPTER 10

EEO AUDIT BRINGS HOPE

Physical symptoms of stress – headaches and digestive problems – were increasing in frequency and severity. Several times Kay became sick on her way to work and had to pull off the highway. She often had strange floating sensations. Sleep deprivation was making her look and feel tired. Sudden and urgent trips to the restroom were uncomfortable and hard to manage in a hostile work environment.

A week had passed since Karl demanded more explanation memos — the ones he wanted before Kay received the day of suspension. She hoped the regional audit team being there all week would keep his mind off her temporarily.

It was obvious Karl and Earl went through Kay's

work when she was out of the office. About two weeks earlier, a post-it note she had stuck to the desktop on a far corner underneath a stack of filing had been moved to a front corner on the top of some other papers. One of them had to have moved it into plain sight because Karl came in immediately, pointed to it and said, "I turned this over," as if he had found it right side up.

Later the same day when Kay told Glenda about it, Glenda said, "He's getting ready to write you up again."

Kay had almost forgotten about the second thing he wanted "explained," the time Karl said an inmate had picked up a roster in his office. Karl never did say what roster it was or show her what he was talking about.

A regional audit involves everyone in the institution. Each department has a visiting team consisting of the respective regional administrator and a supervisory person in the same area from another prison. Education's audit was conducted by Chuck Yates from the region and Gary Hamilton, education supervisor from another facility.

Originally from St. Louis, Gary began his career with the prison system at the medical center. Back then he and Kay called themselves the "tokens" of the department – a black man and a woman.

Tom, Glenda, Dan and Kay planned to discuss Kay's situation with Gary alone while he was at the prison.

"Bet Karl's ticked off that we all know Gary. He'll probably try to keep him away from you," said Tom to Kay.

As if he read their minds, Karl had already warned them the week before, "I'd better not hear of anyone in this department talking to Gary Hamilton or anyone else from the regional office while that audit team is here."

"I'll discuss our problem with Gary if I have to go to his motel," Dan emphatically told Kay. "Karl has no right to try to control who we talk to."

Gary told Tom when they met briefly Monday that everywhere he went in the institution people told him to "talk to education people." At least thirty people had already given him the word. Also, if Gary didn't see Kay before they audited the office Thursday, he would definitely spend some time alone with her then. He wanted Yates to hear what she had to say and emphasized that Karl would not be allowed in.

Kay's hope that the audit team's presence would keep Karl out of her hair turned out to be a pipe dream. He was just keeping a low profile until about 11 am when he gave her an ultimatum.

"You have 60 minutes to give me the two memos I asked for last week." He paused a moment, then added. "You heard what I said. And you better not be doing personal memos on government time."

That demand was impossible since the next hour was all government time, but she said nothing. As he exited the department, the look of pleasure on his face shot through her like a poison dart.

Tom said he had a feeling Karl would get around to the memo sooner or later.

"I've checked with the union officers and a

couple of other stewards for advice. This is what you write: 'I do not remember the specifics of the incidents you are referring to.' Reference it 'Requested memo' and sign your name." He added, "I'd love to see his face when he gets it."

The plan was that Kay would keep out of sight and watch since the 60 minutes would be up when the department closed just before her lunch break. She knew he would come back in an hour to see if she had complied with his order. Kay laughed out loud for the first time in weeks as she typed, then printed and laid it in Karl's mailbox.

She took her lunch into the library down the hall. With the light off and the library door barely open, he would not detect her presence.

As predicted, his key in the lock signaled his arrival. Through the crack in the door Kay had a clear view of the mailbox panel as Karl made a bee line for it. It took only a second. As he read, his face and neck turned crimson. In a rage, he "spiked" the rest of his mail on the table, took that one piece of paper, stomped out and slammed the door.

Kay could hardly wait to tell Tom who laughed and said, "He's probably already up in Wayne's office."

First thing the next morning Glenda called to ask Kay if she could possibly get away long enough to meet with the team auditing the EEO Program. "They want to talk to some of the people I'm counseling," she explained.

Stressed to the point of not thinking rationally, Kay didn't care anymore what Karl did. She would get it anyway. She told only Dan and left with the cart at the scheduled time to pick up the mail.

Glenda and the auditors were waiting. Their team consisted of the Regional EEO administrator and the program administrator at a Chicago facility. After introductions, they explained they had asked Glenda not to preview her cases for them because they wanted to get it directly from the person involved.

The woman auditor asked Kay what kind of problem she had been having. "Just start at the beginning and bring us up to date," she said.

Kay began by saying she had been harassed by "this woman hater" ever since a few minutes after his arrival and none of her sincere diplomatic efforts had improved the situation.

What's this guy's name?" asked the man from Chicago.

Upon hearing Karl Greiner's name, they both groaned, rolled their eyes and said in unison, "Oh, no! Not him again!"

"You mean he hasn't learned his lesson yet? I thought we'd heard the last of him when they kicked him out of Leavenworth," exclaimed the male auditor.

While reviewing bizarre events of the past several months, Kay constantly wrung her hands, smoothed her clothes, "polished" the chair arms and slid her hands back and forth on the tabletop as if scraping up imaginary crumbs. Tears welled up in her eyes several times.

"You are definitely well into the first stages of stress," stated the woman. "You should seek professional help to retain your sanity or you won't survive until the EEO complaint is settled."

The man agreed and told her to "think strong."

Kay felt better after that meeting. These people were not directly involved but readily had recognized that the problem was with Karl, not her.

"That creep has really made a name for himself," said Glenda. She then added that the chaplain from one of Karl's previous institutions was there on that department's audit, and he also wanted to talk to Kay. He remembers Karl well and might help them.

This conversation also turned out to be very uplifting.

Early in the week of the audit Kay found Earl at her desk using the computer. And he had an inmate in there with him. He gave no indication of ever moving, so she asked him how much longer he would need to be there. He ignored her question, just got up in a huff, jerked the computer around, began pulling plugs and cords. In other words, acting like the proverbial spoiled brat. She asked him to please not do that as things were arranged the way they worked best.

"You tell 'em," said the prisoner under his breath. He was a little nervous knowing the office was off limits.

After that obnoxious display, Earl plopped down in another chair and continued on Kay's computer with the inmate standing behind him.

For once, luck was shining down on Kay. Who should walk in at that very moment but Karl and the regional auditors. What could Earl say? He was caught red-handed with an inmate in the office in full view of the regional men.

"I had to show him something," was his feeble response to Karl's inquiring look. The inmate made a hasty exit.

Gary came over to where Kay was making copies. When Karl noticed them, he shot out of the office leaving Yates in mid-sentence and positioned himself near enough to overhear anything they might say.

The next day the prisoner who Earl had in the office came to the door and said, "Ms. Richards, I want to warn you. I've heard some things and I've seen some real strange activities. You really ought to take steps to protect yourself, you know, from Mr. Norman and Mr. Greiner."

When she asked for specifics, he replied, "Just things. Them talking about doing things and what will happen to you. You need to take serious steps now to protect yourself. You're a real nice lady and none of us inmates want anything bad to happen to you. You've got to be real careful."

His warning was clear and chilling.

Kay appreciated his concern. Like many others behind bars, he was a good person who had either made a mistake in judgement or, perhaps, was under the influence of drugs or alcohol at the time of his offense.

Tom called to say the union was ready to serve Wayne with a complaint to the Unfair Labor Relations Board citing Karl Greiner on three counts of "denying union representation to an employee who feels threatened during a disciplinary action."

I'm serving him at 3:45 on a Friday afternoon just like they always do to us," he said. "Then we'll invoke arbitration to the one-day suspension at the same time and day next week."

Dan commented that Karl and Earl would have a hard time backing out of all these complaints. Tom and Kay should bring in as many arbitrators as possible, he added.

Before the union went public through the press, if necessary, in the hope it would put an end to the discrimination, Tom and some of the other guys would explain to Kay's husband what was going on.

A supervisor must charge an employee with an alleged infraction within three weeks. The time limit was nearly up since Karl had asked her to explain the last two events. According to her journal the note thing happened one day before the inmate allegedly went to his office for the nonexistent copy.

Dan came in to tell Kay he had just talked with the auditors alone, surprised that Karl had let them out of his sight. They approached Dan in the hall and asked him if he had any concerns.

His candid response, "Yes, I do. When are you going to get that son-of-a-bitchin' Greiner off our backs?"

At that the auditors about cracked up. They then said they were aware of their problem and would do anything they possibly could from their end to alleviate it.

Thursday morning finally arrived. Hamilton and Yates came into Kay's office about 8:30 and closed the door behind them. They began with the usual audit questions such as what her duties were and how she performed them. After about 10 minutes,

Gary slid his ballpoint pen into his shirt pocket and laid down his yellow legal tablet.

"OK. Now that we have the essentials taken care of, let's get down to brass tacks," he said. "Kay, we want to hear it from you. Tell us about it. All the nitty-gritty. Everything. What is going on here?"

She began with the moment she first met Karl and described events and how the workplace atmosphere had deteriorated during the time he had been their supervisor. She brought out Earl's part and the fact that administration had done nothing to help her.

"You are substantiating what we already know," said Gary. "Practically everybody in this joint has told us what he's doing to you, but any corrective action must begin with you."

They were aware of her EEO claim, and Tom had filled them in on union efforts in her behalf.

Gary then told her Karl had a long history of that kind of behavior.

"You've got to hang in there," said Gary who then became very serious. "You are stronger than he is. Remember that. And be patient. You can outlast him; I know you can! Everything will be OK eventually."

Tom stopped by at lunch to tell Kay about a conversation he'd had with Gary.

"The Bureau has sanctioned Karl every time he got himself in trouble, but they are about fed up with him," Gary had told him.

Before coming to his present position, Karl had been downgraded and disciplinary transferred from Leavenworth. He was told by his superiors at that time, "If you go down to Springfield and keep your nose clean, you might be able to retire on schedule."

He certainly had *not* done that. He began on Kay the minute he stepped in the door.

The auditors left right after lunch on Friday. She felt comforted by their support and encouragement. She began to believe that none of what was going on was her fault.

She prayed she would not see Karl and Earl the rest of the day, but she might as well have wished for the moon. At 3:30, Karl arrogantly ordered her to report to his office "right now. I have another proposal letter to give you."

She called Tom.

"Don't you set foot in that office unless he lets you have a union rep," he cautioned. "In fact, I think I'll call Greiner myself."

Tom quickly called back and said Karl had to confer with someone else regarding the request to accompany her. The other person turned out to be Wayne.

"Greiner insists that nothing will be said to you," said Tom. "All he's going to do is hand you the letter. What's Robbins doing in there anyway? I never heard of a personnel man being present at this stage. Guess Karl's afraid to act without Wayne there to back him up. Or maybe they've given Karl an ultimatum not to give you anything without one of them being there. Just go in, sign your name and walk out."

That is exactly what she did; took her copy and left.

With windows and doors open in every building

on a warm breezy day, the underground corridors were like a wind tunnel. A gust caught the door as it closed. Slam! Kay's shattered nerves caused her to jump, but then she laughed to herself because they probably thought she had slammed the door on purpose.

She was almost crying into the phone, "Tom, this time he wants to give me 21 days off without pay for three offences."

He wrote that she had an inmate distribute sensitive material, sent him to retrieve it, then wrote a computer code on a piece of paper and left it in plain view on her desk.

"There's not a shred of truth to any of it," she said.

Tom said, "You'd think he'd at least wait till the auditors got a few miles down the road," Tom said. "If I have to camp outside the warden's office all night, I'm going to have a talk with him, man to man."

Before he hung up, he added, "Yep, I think it's about time to bring out the Big Gun."

From then on Karl would not do anything official to Kay unless Wayne or someone was with him. It appeared that Karl now realized he had bitten off more than he could chew.

They believed he now recognized the strength and determination of their union people as well as Kay's strong constitution. They would not go down without a fight.

Karl steadfastly refused to meet with Tom one-on-one or even two-on-two (he and Wayne, Tom and Kay).

Tom served Wayne with the Unfair Labor complaint that evening.

Kay had concerns as to her status with the government if she got the 21-day suspension. One worry was if her insurance would be any good if someone in her family had an emergency. Turns out it was solid.

She made up her mind to enjoy the one-day off she received for one of the last false charges. She would try not to worry about the possibility Karl's latest false charges would probably mean she'd get three weeks off or even think about what was going on at work. Family activities were relaxing, and she was able to enjoy being with them. But she couldn't shake the haunting thoughts of having to return to the medical center.

Kay loved the outdoors and just being outside in the bright warm sunshine was good medicine. Sometimes naming the weeds she pulled from her garden and flower beds relieved some of her anxiety.

One straggly weed with beady little seeds looked just like Earl. Yank! Toss. "So long, Snitch." An ugly one with prickly thorns… Karl. Stomp!

Built up frustration came out as anger toward the pesky invaders, but by summer's end, she had become so ill that nothing seemed to work.

She had been in the office only a short time Wednesday morning after the suspension day when one of inmate printers arrived on the job. As they walked down the hall to the print shop, the inmate said, "While you were off, I heard Greiner and Norman talking about you."

She wanted to hear about it so he continued. "Yeah, I was outside your office door waiting for someone to let me in the print shop. They were talking inside, but the door was open about a foot so I could hear them real clear. Mr. Greiner was goin' 'We've got to keep our stories straight.' Then Mr. Norman said somethin' about how he thought that EEO thing was goin' to be a simple matter but apparently, it's bigger and more complicated than he thought. Then Greiner went, 'I don't think she can get that last report I wrote on Friday in to the EEO.'"

He said they paid no attention to him, but they knew he was there because they could see him. Later he gave Kay a written statement about what he had overheard.

When she returned to her office, Tom was waiting to discuss the non-existent progress on her performance evaluation grievance. Karl had used a loophole in the evaluation policy to get around the fact he had not been the department's supervisor long enough to do their yearly evaluations. All the men received good ratings; Kay's was terrible.

But as Tom said, "His real motive for using that obscure rule was to enable him to do yours in order to shoot you down."

Tom had tried several times to talk to Karl about Kay's evaluation but was met with refusals like, "I'm not wasting 'staff time' talking to the union."

When he was finally able to make a futile attempt in person, Karl would not yield one iota. He arrogantly stated, "If I change anything on that evaluation, I'll lower some of those areas."

After that encounter, Tom suggested that maybe they should consider dropping the evaluation thing and put all their emphasis on getting the trumped-up charges dropped.

"Let's get that pay back and your record cleared."

She had come out "Satisfactory" in spite of him. He had written ridiculous statements and marked her as low as possible in every area. But he couldn't give her enough bad scores to bring the average down low enough make it "unsatisfactory." He could not beat the excellent and outstanding ratings she received in areas over which he had no control.

There was a vast difference between this evaluation and the great rating Jim gave her just before he retired. One of the more asinine statements Karl made was his admonishment of Kay for not using carbon paper instead of making copies. No one had used carbon paper around there for years.

Her special commendation in the monthly Central Office Status Report from D.C. regarding her submission of error-free education data was not even mentioned. She had the highest performance rating and lowest error ratio for all the Bureau facilities in the entire country. Karl had ignored the whole thing and just put a copy of it in her mailbox without comment.

The special honor was not entered on her "Significant Incident Log" either. Both positive and negative aspects of an employee's performance are supposed to be noted. Everything Karl wrote on Kay's was either a lie or stupid like not using carbon paper. Everything negative.

It appeared that Karl came into the office for one reason only—to yell at Kay. Once it went like this, "You will not delegate up!"

Her silence and puzzled look just brought on more.

"Must I remind you constantly that you are the lowest graded person in this department, and you will write all the passes, do all clerical work, make and answer all calls, you will not refer callers to another number. You are the receptionist! Did you get that? You will not delegate up!"

Apparently, Dan had done her a favor by writing a pass for an inmate rather than have him interrupt her.

Dan apologized later stating, "Earl must have seen me. I wanted to help, not get you into more trouble."

At lunch, Tom munched on his sandwich while turning through the papers in the newest proposal file. He paused and chuckled. "Here's your memo. 'I do not remember the specifics of the incidents you are referring to.' I love it."

Tom believed that the increase in sabotage lately meant they were laying the groundwork for their next plan of action.

"They've not been successful so far in getting you on security violations, so they're about to activate Plan B – attack your performance," he said.

CHAPTER 11

THE BIG GUN

Tom's belief that the campaign against Kay was moving into a new phase seemed accurate. Some very strange things were happening lately.

Papers were showing up in weird places, like a printing order that vanished for three weeks just to turn up in the print shop right after the foreman sent a duplicate.

A letter to the regional office disappeared from Kay's desk and showed up in the warden's office. Two inmate files and a lot of loose filing disappeared. About 2,000 pamphlets went out before they were collated, apparently because someone had told them to come get them.

Karl yelled at Kay about this over the phone

while another supervisor listened. At that time, she didn't even know the uncollated booklets had been picked up.

Computer entries were messed up or changed. Like the time Kay found about 100 new admissions she had put on callout to go to the chapel came out on computer to go to the gym. She caught this potential mess in the nick of time and changed them back to the right location. She remembered that Earl was at the computer when she arrived that morning.

Tom had his unique way of describing any situation. "Karl's got his toenails dug in."

The appointment with Warden Preston was at the usual time – 3:30 on Friday afternoon. Depressed and discouraged, Kay dreaded it, but Tom was raring to go. He had held back "the Big Gun" for several weeks and enthusiastically anticipated the impact of his secret weapon.

Wayne told Glenda she could not attend this meeting. He agreed that her moral support was needed: "Yes, Lord only knows Kay needs all the support she can get, but 'disciplinaries' are union matters," he said.

Given the option to write a memo, Glenda wrote directly to the warden.

Even armed with the Big Gun, Kay grew more apprehensive as the formal hearing date approached. Everyone knew she was innocent and Karl's charges asinine, but that fact had not prevented punishment being levied against her yet.

The first thing the warden asked for was a copy of whatever it was Kay allegedly distributed. Of course, Karl could not produce it.

In his statement, Tom brought out that the note was left stuck onto the desk under a pile of other papers and was moved by someone while Kay was out of the office. The code had nothing to do with work, and it could not have been read from the hall even if it had been left where Karl claims it was found. He then emphasized there was no evidence to back up the charge that the alleged roster with the computer codes on it ever existed.

When the warden asked if there was anything else anyone wished to add, Tom said, "Yes, I have one more memo to submit."

He went across the room and handed him the Big Gun.

Dead silence. All eyes were fixed on Warden Preston. As he read, a concerned expression slowly spread across his face as Dan's serious truthful words leaped from the page.

"Kay Richards has been the object of administrative harassment for a number of months. Much of this is due to the fact she is a woman and has the lowest GS grade in an all-male department. She has the kind of personality that desires to please and is not afraid to walk the extra mile.

"Kay Richards has been the object of harassment from Karl Greiner, Education Supervisor, and Earl Norman, Teacher. Currently much of the harassment is due to a demand of changing procedures. Changes are always given in a confusing manner with Karl Greiner later denying that the order was ever given or rescinding what was previously ordered and not informing Kay. His

orders are always given in a profane and irritable manner.

"I once overheard Karl Greiner and Earl Norman discussing that they needed to 'get rid of Kay Richards.' I warned Kay early in the spring of this year that the current effort by Karl Greiner and Earl Norman was to put her in a compromising position which would eventually cause her to lose her job.

"By his own admission, Karl Greiner is confused and frustrated most of the time by departmental functions. It is this writer's opinion that Karl Greiner is totally unfit to manage people, much less a specialized department. Signed, Dan Williams"

When he finished reading, Preston looked directly at Kay and their eyes met momentarily. In that split second, she saw gentleness in those eyes. The look of concern never left his face, but he asked no more questions. After a few moments of silence, he said everyone would be notified as soon as he made a decision in the matter.

Tom was happy as they went down the front steps. "I do believe the Big Gun had the desired effect," he said. "Did you see Wayne? Before we could get out the door, he practically leaped from his chair clear across the room to Preston's desk to get his hands on it."

Even though Tom, and even Kay, felt good about it, she had been beaten down emotionally for so long, she couldn't get her hopes up even though she tried.

A week later the response time limit for the warden's decision was almost up and they had not heard a word. Then out of the blue one morning, Wayne appeared in the hall outside Kay's office with a paper in his hand.

Kay expected that his purpose for being there was to bring the final draft of the minutes for her approval and signature. Instead, he greeted her with a smile and said as he handed her a memo, "We didn't do any more to the minutes because the warden has decided to drop this matter entirely!"

"Did I hear him right?" she asked herself.

His words went around in her head like a whirlwind. It took a minute to fully register. This was the first justice she had received since Karl arrived. Somehow, she managed to sign for the letter and thank Wayne.

He started to leave but paused and commented, "I've never seen or heard of anything like the support you have from people in this institution. More than exceptional. It's phenomenal!"

Word got back to Tom, Glenda and Kay that at least three dozen employees had gone on her behalf to the warden and/or to Wayne. It was very emotional to learn all those people had vouched for her. In the meantime, there was no denying that it would probably be just a matter of time before Karl struck again.

It was a good time to share the good news with Glenda. She stepped into Glenda's office while making her daily run to the mailroom.

Without comment, she handed the memo to Glenda, who read down to the part that said, *"After careful consideration... as well as information that came to light during your oral response, I find the charge and specifications not supported. Accordingly, it is my decision to close this file with no action taken."*

As if pulled together by magnets, Kay and Glenda embraced each other and cried.

"Finally," Glenda sobbed. "Kay's got something to feel happy about."

Karl was not expecting to lose so it came as quite a shock, but there was no change in him or Earl after the last case was thrown out. It was as if they thought themselves invincible and the loss only a minor setback.

They were already working on their next plot before the ink dried on the warden's decision.

Kay had seen Earl go into Karl's office with a two-inch thick file. She found out later he had been compiling her "mistakes." These turned out to be student information he had given her, changed it the next day and then complained to Karl about her errors. Since he left everything laying in plain sight, Kay was able to make copies of them.

They were launching a last-ditch effort but at least, they finally had a warden who would listen. Preston had even asked Karl why he kept bringing him cases without any evidence. But the Big Gun was what really got the warden's attention.

As time went on, the prisoners' concern for Kay became evident. Things witnessed by workers and students were unbelievable. Word always travels rapidly through the inmate "grapevine" and they naturally identify with the underdog. One day she realized that there was constantly at least one worker or student in the classroom reading or studying when she was in the office. They had become her self-appointed protectors.

And for good reason. Karl's campaign continued.

One day, he came through the door demanding to know, "Who was that officer that was in here?"

Surprised, Kay hesitated.

By then Karl was right in her face. "You tell me who that officer was!"

"You mean early this morning?" she asked, thinking to herself that Earl had to have told Karl there had been a unit officer there to deliver a message to Kay from Tom.

"Yes," he snarled.

She told him the officer's name.

"What did he want?"

"He brought me a message."

"What about?" When she hesitated, he yelled, "I asked you a question!"

"A personal matter."

"I'm asking you what you were talking about."

When Kay stood her ground, he became even more agitated. "Are you going to tell me what that officer was telling you or not?"

"No."

At that point, Karl shut the office door and turned back to her.

"Kay, you work for me from 7:30 to 4, and I expect to be informed of who you talk to and what you talk about."

She was firm. "I don't have to reveal personal matters to anyone at any time."

Angrier still, he retorted, "Are you saying it's

none of my business what you were talking about while you are on duty?"

"It was my personal conversation and it's no one else's business no matter what time it is." She surprised herself with her assertive burst.

Karl would not maintain eye contact with her even for a split second.

Then his voice took on a strange tone — a bit quieter. "Kay, you get a little salty lately when I ask you questions."

"Considering what you're doing to me, I'm supposed to be all hearts and flowers?" she asked.

"It's not my concern whether or not you're at ease with me. My concern is what's going on in this department. You say you don't have time to pull up that daily roster by 7:45, and I don't want you talking to other people while on duty."

The roster in question was not even available until about 8 each morning.

He went on and on and on, then added, "And I saw you wasting time in the hall with that same man the other day."

Kay almost had to laugh. That was the day the basement was flooded after a heavy rain and people were waiting in the corridor for the ankle-deep water to be pumped out so they could be cleared to enter that building. The officers had just changed shifts, and the one Karl was referring to was on his way to his post as well.

Karl had cursed at her at the time for refusing to enter the office, also in the basement, before the water was gone. "Earl is already in there at your computer."

Kay said flatly, "If he's crazy enough to operate electrical equipment in six inches of water, more power to him, no pun intended. But I'm sure not going to."

"I'm giving you an order. You will not now or at any time in the future talk to anyone unless I say so!" He turned and left without another word.

Tom and Glenda confirmed for her that an employee cannot be forced to reveal personal information to a superior. Neither can a subordinate be prevented from talking to anyone else without the supervisor's permission.

That same day the computer teacher came back in after lunch and found, to Kay's surprise, that an inmate had been locked in with her. The prisoner explained that Earl had approved his staying in to work during the lunch hour.

He was so quiet. To say she would have been startled had he come out of that classroom is an understatement. It was intentional because she remembered the smug look Earl gave her through the glass as he left for lunch.

"I wonder why he did that," said the teacher. "Earl knows the dangers of a stunt like that. It's a good thing that inmate's not assaultive."

Earl had also left a copy machine repairman alone with a bunch of inmates the day Kay was on suspension. The next time the repairman was there he told her that one inmate was especially interested in his tools. This made him so nervous that he locked his toolbox and waited until Dan came in. A strictly enforced policy states that outside people "must be under escort at all times" for their own safety as well as to protect the government from lawsuits.

A few days later Kay arrived at work to find her computer had vanished and a different one sat in its place. As a last resort, she asked Karl.

"It's none of your damn business where it is or why it's gone," he snapped in his usual hateful tone.

A few minutes later, he demanded that a lengthy report be done immediately on the unfamiliar computer. It took longer on the much older computer. Karl didn't need it immediately either, maybe not at all, because it was still untouched in his mailbox several days later.

The computer was nowhere to be found. Kay had given up the search the next day when an inmate told her that Karl had him carry it to his office the evening before she found it missing. But it was no longer there and could not be found anywhere in the institution. Tom, Glenda, Dan and Kay all believed Karl stole it, but they had no proof except the inmate's statement.

The Unfair Labor Relations Investigator scheduled his hearing for the middle of September. Tom explained that the investigator takes statements from all those directly involved. With arbitration (as in Kay's case) the employee can observe the entire session as well as call all witnesses he or she desires.

Labor investigators generally side with management unless it can be proven without a shadow of a doubt the claim is valid. Also, the administration's policy is to automatically back management in disciplinary cases. Otherwise some employees would walk all over the good supervisors who would have no control.

At the hearing and after Earl had given his statement, Wayne came into the room where Tom and Kay were waiting to testify. He asked Kay if she would be interested in a vacant position as a medical supply clerk.

"I appreciate you asking but I'm not qualified for that job," she said. "Besides, Karl threatened to block any attempt I might make to transfer."

Wayne assured, "Karl has no say in this. I can place you there as a trainee at your same grade and pay. By the time the trainee period is up you would be qualified as well as receive a raise in pay. You have a few days to think about it."

He explained he could do anything he wanted with a position, and the warden had already mentioned the possibility of moving her away from Karl. Also, Karl had already been informed of the fact he would have no say or control in this action, and it upset him terribly.

Just prior to Dan coming in to testify to the labor investigator, he overheard Karl and Earl discussing this new development. Karl was adamant when he emphatically declared, "I don't want her moved. I want her fired!"

Karl called a staff meeting later in the week. Kay was required to attend and take notes but not allowed even the common courtesy of speaking or being acknowledged.

"I have something very important to discuss," Karl stated as he passed out memos to each person. "I have sorted out responsibilities within this department and rearranged some to make for a more efficient and smoother running operation," he went on with an air of superiority.

He rearranged them, all right... moved nearly everything under Kay's name. Almost every routine task except actual classroom teaching was added to her already unbelievable workload.

Of the men, Dan got the worst of it — all evenings with the extra tasks that went along with that shift — payback for his support of Kay. The other men came out with fewer extra duties, but Earl had only his basic education class.

Tom said Karl was getting in a few extra jabs while he still had Kay in his clutches. Kick her a few more times.

One of the new duties on Kay's list was the "law run" which would keep her out of the office where she was supposed to do "everything unaided" almost two half-days per week. It involved checking in and out and delivering law books and materials to inmates unable to come to the law library. Areas included lock-up, quarantined wards and isolation.

Tom said, "Karl is making it even harder on you because we brought the unfair labor people down on their heads." He laughed, "I'd like to tell him that if he didn't like that one, just stick around because we've got more."

Strange, but true, was the fact that Karl's "friends" did not even like or trust him. Another new supervisor in the psychiatric unit who had known Karl for years warned Tom, "Watch Greiner. He's a snake and will snitch you off in a second."

On the way out one afternoon, Karl and that

same man were just a few feet ahead of Glenda and Kay in the key line. They were making a lot of noise, joking, laughing and generally acting like fools.

Then in the sally port, they kept right on even though the women were less than two feet away. The other supervisor said, "Why don't you just put your arm around her and..."

Karl interrupted, "Tell you what... I'm not going to give her to you. I'm just going to..." He wiggled his eyebrows, nudged the other man in the ribs and they both snickered.

Everybody in there heard it. He was so blatant. Other employees forced to listen were uncomfortable, but it made Kay feel awful.

Glenda said when they were outside, "The jerk's terrible, but the more people who see him in action, the better."

The next morning Wayne's assistant brought Kay a typed memo to sign requesting the new position. It seemed strange that she had to ask for the job since Wayne was placing her there but apparently, it was part of the paperwork needed to clear the trainee position with Washington.

The move would be bittersweet, but Kay would work halfway across the institution from Karl. Everyone encouraged her saying that things would be better. She wanted so much to believe that Karl couldn't hurt her anymore, but she did not have peace about it.

On her last day in education, Dan reflected the consensus as she was picking up her personal things. "I'm sure sorry to see you go, but it's best that you're getting away from here before you crack up. Seriously, if you don't get relief from this, you'll end up in the hospital."

He was interrupted by a boisterous, "Hallelujah! She can't do the job anyway!" It was Earl who then made a quick exit. He had been ignoring the others as he appeared to be reading a piece of his mail.

"Boy, what a bad attitude," said Dan.

"What's the matter with him anyway," asked the small engines teacher whose classroom was in another building and had not witnessed the harassment.

Dan presented Kay with a card and a generous gift certificate signed by everyone in the department except Karl and Earl. "We didn't ask them," volunteered Ben.

During the day every one of them, except the same two, came by again to personally say they were going to miss her and how much they appreciated her. All expressed concern for her health recognizing recent physical problems were related to the stressful situation. Some of them tried to make her feel better by clowning around and making lighthearted comments.

She was overcome by their concern and thoughtfulness.

CHAPTER 12

SAME SONG, DIFFERENT BAND

Kay never expected to work in Medical Supply. She enjoyed her job in education and would have worked there until retirement but was thankful to get away from Karl.

Stress was taking its toll. She was in a perpetual daze, never knowing what the next few weeks held in store.

It was as though the institution had become a pre-retirement gathering place for the good ol' boys. Many of Karl's clique were there, and his tentacles reached into every department throughout the prison. He had a way of intimidating people, and their "code" was strong like they all belonged to the same lodge.

Kay adapted quickly to the new duties but felt

uneasy. From Day One, she had strong adverse vibrations after transferring to medical supply. But Tom remained hopeful that removing her from Karl's grip would improve the situation.

A strange unwelcome feeling enveloped her, especially in the presence of Warren Crowe, the pudgy, sloppy, smelly man who was supervisor of medical supply. His practical nurse license had lapsed which labeled him irresponsible.

Tom learned through the union that Warren's office clerk Debby Milford had wanted the supply clerk job. But he'd been told by his supervisor that the job was Kay's and he should go along with that decision.

It was hard to tell what Debby's job was. A mousey overweight woman in her late twenties, she called herself Warren's "secretary." They often spent time in the office playing around with the computers, including video gaming.

Debby seemed to have no set hours. She was very imposed upon when asked to cover the supply area a few minutes even though her main activity seemed to be writing personal letters, filling out Christmas cards, reading magazines and compiling two three-inch thick recipe notebooks on the office computer on government time. Kay could not understand why she had bad feelings toward her. Except Kay had the job she wanted.

Meryl Simms, a practical nurse in the units, was assigned to medical supply on regular rotation. An attractive divorcee in her early thirties, she would in the months to come provide Kay with invaluable information and warnings, because Warren and

Debby talked a lot in her presence.

People in Karl's clique were older and more devious with their underhanded plots. Warren, a toady who desperately wanted the prestige that he believed that group represented, greedily fell for the enticement of a larger space and new equipment offered to him as payment as bribery for his help with their vendetta.

Warren had previously been friendly to her when he brought printing orders to education. But the atmosphere changed diametrically when Kay moved to supply.

Meryl filled in some blanks regarding Warren's issues from what she had overheard in the supply area. It was no excuse for his behavior, but it did help explain his conduct to know that his childhood had been unstable. His parents had no real home, never worked, just traveled all over the country and took handouts from churches and charities in every town they went through. As a child he had often been sent in first to gain sympathy from those agencies.

That could explain why he hated anything to do with church or religion. And from his comments, it seemed he disliked his own wife and young daughter and was trying to figure out a way to dump them, Meryl said.

No one could guess what Debby's problem was. Or why. She had no personality, craved approval and found fault with others.

The supply area was crowded and congested. Medical and surgical supplies on metal racks were stacked to the ceiling with barely enough space between them to push supply carts. The adjoining sterilization room held autoclaves, metal tables, drying racks and a huge dishwasher. A small room next to it was where they decontaminated equipment, cleaned and washed surgical instruments before sterilization. A larger space and newer equipment were badly needed.

Across the hall was a ten-foot square room that housed the on-line oxygen set up and other gases for the hospital. Included were three 300-gallon liquid oxygen tanks, four 100-gallon reserve tanks and several small portable units.

Meryl or Kay checked the oxygen supply at least three times daily. As soon as an oxygen tank became empty, it was replaced by the supplier downtown. Normal usage was less than one tank per week which always left at least two full ones available at all times.

It was evident that Warren's intention was to confuse Kay, but it was also affecting Meryl. Whenever things began to run smoothly, he changed everything. For example, inventory was kept on computer with orders deducted as soon as possible after delivery. One morning none of the commands worked. Meryl and Kay were trying to determine what had happened when Debby came prancing through complaining about having to correct all the errors they had made on inventory sheets.

"Of course, we made mistakes," exclaimed Meryl. "How could we help it? You could have at least told us you changed everything."

During the next few weeks, there were attempts

to get Kay on security violations. But these perpetrators were not quite as sophisticated as Karl and Earl.

Kay had a strong feeling she was being set up again—the same sensation that had plagued her ever since transferring to medical supply. Perhaps her concerns were connected to all the new equipment Warren had received and stored in a promised larger area.

Meryl preferred the earlier shift so she could be home when her kids got out of school. Kay preferred a later shift so she could get her kids to school after her husband left for work early, and he could be home when they got home. At first, it did not matter to Warren, but he later made specific assigned weekly schedules of work times and duties.

Each unit had a "detail pouch" containing daily notices for that particular department as well as a passbook to use if an inmate was on call out to be gone for an appointment during work hours. The pouches were placed by the sally port to be picked up by the first person from each area who arrived at work.

One morning Medical Supply had two passbooks in their pouch. Meryl said to ignore it because the officers will see the extra and take it out the next day. But the extra remained a few weeks.

Not long afterward during one of Kay's early weeks they traded shifts, per Warren's approval, because Meryl needed to be off early. When Meryl picked up the pouch it contained only one passbook. She commented to Kay that the extra must have been discovered.

About mid-morning Warren stood in the door with an investigative lieutenant. He held up a passbook asked whose responsibility was to pick it up.

Meryl volunteered, "The first one here each morning."

Warren was becoming agitated. "Who picked it up this morning?"

"I did," said Meryl.

Warren's surprise was obvious. "Go with the lieutenant and make a statement," he said to Meryl.

When Meryl returned, she exclaimed. "You'll never believe what *that* was all about!"

She went on to explain that an inmate found the passbook under the mat in the sally port when mopping the floor. It was clear back underneath, so it had to have been placed there intentionally.

"I bet Warren placed it there on his way out last night because he had asked me why I came in early this morning instead of you." Meryl said, reminding him he had ok'd it himself the day before. He never mentioned the incident again.

Another time two surgical instruments went missing from a suture set being sterilized. In a prison setting, that is a serious matter. When Kay noticed they were gone, one of the inmate workers said he had found them in the hall and turned them in to Warren who just dropped them in his desk drawer.

Incidents were happening rapidly – first one thing, then another – like the disappearance of all the rubber safety gloves from the decontamination room. Warren finally brought some enormous thick black elbow-length "things" that felt and looked like inner tubes. It was impossible to work in them, so they continued to wear two or three layers of exam gloves.

Warren also was deliberately giving Kay erroneous information about the oxygen supply. He first said the gauges on top of the tanks indicated the amount of oxygen still in the tank.

Later she asked Meryl why the gauges on the empty tank read the same as full ones. Meryl explained that the gauges only showed tank and line pressure and when a tank got low, the system automatically switched to another. The ice around the spigot on top indicated which tank was presently being pulled from. In case of an emergency and all three big tanks became empty, the system automatically switched to the four 100-gallon reserve bank which would activate a red alarm light on the wards and in the room.

Then Meryl became very serious. "Be very careful with the oxygen. That's how they're going to get you... with the oxygen."

Kay must have looked puzzled because she added, "Just remember what I'm telling you." She accented every word, *"Watch. The. Oxygen."*

And then there was the key incident. Employees wore safety chains around their waists to which key rings were hooked to keep keys from being dropped, laid down, lost or grabbed by an inmate. One day Kay's keys caught on a wire rack and broke, so she carried them in her pocket the rest of the day.

When time to leave she laid the keys on her purse while putting on her jacket. Who should walk in at that very instant but Debby. She said not a word, just turned and left. The incident was so insignificant Kay hardly remembered it.

About two weeks later Kay got a proposal memo charging her with "Laying down a set of keys" and "Not reporting yourself for violating the security of a set of keys." Punishment – a 15-day suspension.

Debby denied reporting the incident. She and Warren refused to name Kay's accuser which is against policy. "You'll find out if and when we decide to pursue the matter after we get your memo," he said.

There was not enough about it to write the memo they requested. Kay did lay them down for maybe two seconds right in front of her, but that was not a violation, especially given the broken chain and the fact that all inmates were locked on their wards for the 4 o'clock count.

After Kay got the 15-day suspension for laying down keys and not reporting herself, she finally called Tom. He assured her that she had done nothing wrong.

According to the union, no employee had ever been in trouble for simply laying down a set of keys for a few seconds within a few inches of their hands.

Kay admitted later she should have asked for Tom's assistance but was afraid he'd be disappointed in her for getting into "trouble" again so soon after Warden Preston had been kind enough to remove her from Karl's evil grip. However, Tom had known all along as the union gets notice of every disciplinary proposal, but they cannot get involved unless the employee asks for help. He told her later they were waiting and hoping she would seek help as the charge was ridiculous.

"You don't deserve this. I can't believe they actually did this to you for something so insignificant," he said. "Would I ever have loved to have gotten into the middle of this one!"

The union arbitrator scheduled his two-day investigation and hearing into the "inmate holding printer together" incident during the second week of Kay's 15-day suspension.

Worry about losing two weeks' pay was making her even sicker. She still had not been able to bring herself to talk to her family. By then, it was obvious that something was terribly wrong with her.

One afternoon, she took herself to the emergency room with what she thought was appendicitis. It turned out to be stress-related colitis, a chronic condition that will be monitored the rest of her life.

Just like in education, only when Kay alone would be blamed in one of their set-ups did management follow through with disciplinary action. Warren was no doubt taking lessons from Karl.

Karl's hostile workplace and "quid pro quo" sexual harassment had now progressed through vitriol and retaliation to a vicious vendetta.

"Just follow the tentacle," Tom said. "It leads right back to Greiner."

For example, the passbook and missing instrument incidents were dropped, but the "key" thing was prosecuted to the fullest. On top of that, Warren entered every single charge on her significant incident log and yearly evaluation without mention of her exoneration or the charges being dropped.

The performance evaluation that Karl had done on Kay the year before insulted her as a person. Warren ridiculed her intelligence with remarks like, "You think that if you stay late and do a good job, you're supposed to get a good evaluation?" He then echoed Karl saying she was a mediocre employee.

Not until the union intervened did the nursing supervisor agree to raise her overall rating from minimum to satisfactory. But she adamantly refused to change a single area total or rewrite any of those false narrative comments.

That was when Warren arrogantly told Tom, "We're going to fight you."

It never stopped.

Kay became the only employee at the institution required to report in by phone as soon as she arrived on the job with no credit given for any time worked before the call. It came as a surprise to anyone not in on the conspiracy who happened to answer the phone.

Once when Kay was unable to make the call for about thirty minutes, Tom, who was working in the control center that day, had to verify her arrival time. The nursing director hung up on him when he said there were others with him who would also vouch for her.

"We've all decided..." Tom was referring to himself and the other officers in the control room,

"Maybe you should run a red banner up the flagpole when you get here each morning to announce your arrival!"

Kay really appreciated those guys as well as others in the institution who were so supportive.

Another incident began when everyone (except Debby, of course) had to help unload a truckload of supplies that had just arrived. Warren immediately helped himself to the Receiving Department's cookies and motioned toward the "hot cage" saying, "There's something in there for us."

The hot cage held sensitive items like drugs, needles, syringes and other things that only an employee in the ordering department could pick up. Orders received were placed in the locked cage until the appropriate person came to sign for them.

A receiving employee unlocked the cage to let Warren in. He waved the package high, he said loudly so all could hear, "Is the paperwork done on this?"

Someone indicated that it was, so he yelled, "I'm putting this on Kay's cart."

By the time they got back to their area, it was time for Kay to go home so Meryl said she would see that everything was put away.

Kay knew the instant Meryl walked in the next morning that something was wrong. She said that the parcel Warren had placed on Kay's load the day before contained syringes and needles. When they were unloading, she had asked Warren why they had brought a package for Pharmacy, but he did not answer her question, just asked who "actually pushed the cart it was on."

Meryl continued, "I don't want to worry you, but you really ought to know that Warren and the director of nursing made me write a memo about the box after you left."

She had tried to explain to them what had happened, but they forced her to write the memo several times until it suited them, naming Kay as the person who pushed the cart and the contents of the package.

Several violations surrounded this incident, none committed by Kay, but she was the one blamed. First, the receiving employee should never have released it to anyone other than Pharmacy, Tom said. In addition, Warren had no authority to take it out of the cage. By the time Tom talked to the nurse supervisor later in the day, they had already dropped the entire matter.

Meryl overheard Warren telling Debby that the reason it was dropped was "because it would get too many other people in trouble besides Richards" which would have included himself.

He also instructed Debby "not to write any more memos that Kay could call harassment."

They must have either threatened or were blackmailing Meryl because she kept trying to give subtle hints and warnings but seemed to be afraid to openly help Kay anymore.

Kay's second EEO complaint against Karl was ready. She was filing for both "Harassment Due to Sex" and "Retaliation" for filing the first time.

Glenda said, "It's obvious they're really out to get you now since we brought the union arbitrator and labor department down on their heads."

Management claims that filing a grievance is not to be held against an employee, but all employees know better. Kay's saga proved it.

On the day the union arbitrator came regarding the "inmate holding the printer together incident" in education, Tom met Kay at the front entrance with Bill Holden, union arbitration representative. A pleasant man in his early fifties, Holden was experienced in defending employees, and Tom had the utmost confidence in him. Management was represented by Federal Attorney Herbert Tidwell, who had worked at the medical center several years earlier.

The impartial arbitrator was Matthew Cataldi, a retired circuit court judge from Kansas City. The judge began by noting rules and regulations for the hearing. Also, that he would mediate the matter, and his decision would be binding.

Karl was the first to testify. He went on for quite a while about his "concerns" for the security of the computer. Right away there were noticeable contradictions in Karl's testimony.

A big discrepancy was in the way he described the event itself. First, he said Kay was sitting at the computer while the inmate stood by the printer with his hands on the document as it came out. Later, he described the two of them sitting shoulder to shoulder at the computer. He also claimed to have placed an "out of bounds" sign on the door and the screen could be read from the hallway.

Next Warden Preston testified the information being printed was not sensitive. He also quoted Data Coordinator Glenda Potter who had maintained throughout that there was no breach of security as a result of the incident.

Next was Glenda. She explained the screen was hidden and the document was not sensitive, so inmates could be in the room with the computer. She emphasized again that Kay did not commit a breach of security.

Then came the valuable testimony of Dan Williams. He verified that the "out of bounds" sign was ordered and installed after the alleged incident. He also testified about overhearing Karl and Earl discussing that they needed to get rid of Kay.

When Kay's turn came, she explained that the inmate was assigned to her and she had been ordered by Karl not to delegate work or ask assistance from staff. She testified further regarding Karl's claimed urgency in getting the document printed and the inmate's help was essential. He could not see the screen or the keyboard commands as she sat at the computer and he stood behind the printer.

Attorney Tidwell argued that Kay's punishment was justified as security could "possibly" have been breached by the mere fact the inmate was in the room.

Then Holden gave the union's contentions. He entered into the record that it was eight days before Karl mentioned adverse action while he tried to make up his mind on what he was going to do. He brought out Karl's conflicting testimonies noting that Kay's description of the incident was totally different than any of Karl's stories.

He reiterated that Dan backed Kay up regarding

the "out of bounds" sign and that the printer had been sabotaged according to the repairman. He repeated statements by Glenda and Preston that there was no breach of security. He also stressed that management did not refute any of the above or Dan's statement describing Karl's obsessed disdain for Kay. In conclusion, Holden attested that the suspension of one day was unjustified, and it should be removed from her record with all pay and benefits restored.

Last the judge discussed the case. He stressed that arbitrators usually refuse to interfere with management unless the penalty is found to be excessive, unreasonable, capricious or arbitrary. He further stated that arbitrators vary in their opinions of what is excessive, and they do not necessarily agree with management. Also, the burden of proof in discipline cases is always on the employer.

After the hearing Holden said, "Compared with others I've been involved with, it went very well. I believe the judge listened to us and we have a good chance of coming out on top."

The decision was in the union's hands within the required sixty days.

On the last of 21-pages was his decision: *"From the testimony given, it appears to this arbitrator that the testimony of the Superintendent of Education was less that credible on several counts…"*

He went on to mention the diametrically opposing testimonies and unrefuted statements made by Glenda and Dan.

He then concluded: *"Management not having*

proved a breach of institution security, even by a preponderance of the evidence presented, the arbitrator, therefore, is left with no alternative but to grant the grievance of the grievant, Kay Richards. The arbitrator orders management to remove from her personnel record the one-day suspension and requires that the grievant be made whole for all loss of pay and fringe benefits.

"So ordered, Matthew Cataldi, Arbitrator"

CHAPTER 13

THE OXYGEN CHRONICLES

Warren acted very authoritative the morning he handed out new schedules. He was splitting the details which would assign Kay and Meryl specific responsibilities for each two-week period. He emphasized they were to follow the assignments to the letter. They could not trade shifts or areas for each other's convenience without his prior approval.

One detail consisted of supply inventory and distribution while the other involved sterilization, decontamination and maintaining the oxygen supply. The inmates stayed on the same detail.

The women were comfortable with the way it was before – each working together per her own schedule on whatever needed to be done. It was soon evident Warren was laying groundwork so he would know who was responsible for what and when. Another plot was brewing.

Meryl and Kay resolved to watch out for each other at all times.

The division of responsibilities hindered efficiency. Kay drew "supply" in the first rotation which turned out to be uneventful. But things were about to change.

Kay had completed two stints in the supply area and was beginning her second in charge of sterilization, decontamination and oxygen. First thing Monday morning, she checked the oxygen supply. One of the three tanks had been replaced on Friday, and the hospital had used little over the weekend.

She then swept up a dustpan full of cigarette butts and other trash that had been tossed under the door from the hall since Friday. This had become a daily ritual.

The oxygen storage room was at the entrance to a curved tunnel to the next building. Smokers would sneak a puff or two as they walked along the underground connecting tunnel. When the echo of footsteps signaled someone approaching around the next curve, many burning smokes ended up under the first available door. Once a whole smoldering cigarette came sliding in. Explosion and fire danger always exist where chemicals and gases are in use or stored.

A truck driver from the oxygen service company told Kay about a scary incident that happened to a delivery man. A 100-gallon tank had fallen off the back of a truck while being unloaded at another location. The impact broke off the valves which unleashed such power that the tank became a missile. It rocketed through two concrete block walls, shot across a large factory floor full of workers using welding equipment, then crashed into and demolished another concrete wall. The spewing gas under high pressure had made the heavy metal tank behave like a loose balloon. Luckily, no one was hurt.

Warren was on leave all week but early on Wednesday afternoon, he surprised Kay and Meryl by making a brief appearance in the supply area.

Before they could ask, he volunteered, "They called me in. Pharmacy's having computer trouble." He stayed in the pharmacy all afternoon. He didn't come around where they were working again but when Kay left to go home, he was at the computer in his office.

Kay began the usual routine when arriving Thursday morning. After reporting in to the nursing office, she changed into scrubs and was about to check the oxygen when the phone rang. A ward nurse reported their alarm light had come on indicating the oxygen system had gone on reserve. She said there had been no emergency overnight, she just wanted to let them know. Strange. All three LOX tanks were full when Kay checked them before leaving the day before.

When she opened the oxygen storeroom, a wall of steam rolled out. She could see one gigantic "snow cone" through the fog and two ice capped tanks. Oxygen was hissing out a small hole near the top of the snow cone changing to steam as it met the warmer air. Ice had encased that tank. It was obvious that the gas had been escaping for hours. Kay grabbed a large wrench used to hook the tanks to the hospital system. She had to brake and dig out six or eight inches of ice to get her hand in to close the valve. It was wide open.

The alarm light in the room was not on which indicated an ample supply, but all three LOX tanks were empty. Someone with access to the room and familiar with the system had wasted nearly a thousand gallons of liquid oxygen. That person had also tampered with the alarm.

A feeling of imminent danger engulfed her. The cigarette butts! A quick look around revealed the usual ample supply on the floor, but none were burning. Only fate had kept that building full of people from being blown to smithereens.

The valve that had been opened was the one where the supplier fills the tank. It is sealed after each filling, not to be opened until the tank was returned for refilling.

Pieces began to fall into place. Strict duty assignments. Pharmacy computer supposedly on the fritz. Warren remaining after everyone left. A valve deliberately turned on. System alarm sabotaged.

Meryl's warning then hit Kay like a ton of bricks, *"Just remember what I'm telling you, Kay. The oxygen is how they're going to get you."*

Kay went back to the supply room and slumped into the desk chair. Suddenly her realistic dream of 18 months earlier came back to her. She began to tremble.

Only one burning cigarette tossed under the door into that gas-filled room… Just one. And the five-story building would have been reduced to rubble. Many patients and employees would have been killed or injured. Her dream from months earlier was so clear.

Her voice quivered as she said out loud, *"It was both a premonition and a warning!"*

Luck? No.

Devine protection? Pure and simple.

If she had to pinpoint when she finally decided she could take no more, that was it.

She asked herself, "What kind of person cares so little for human life that he would put four or five hundred people in jeopardy for a promotion? Or to get me? What else are these people capable of?"

She realized her own life was also in danger and made the decision she had fought off for months. She would apply for extended sick leave as soon as the HR office opened that very morning. That way she could receive some pay and could keep her group medical insurance.

So ill she did not realize how sick she really was, she wondered why she had taken the abuse so long. But knowing what was going on and that she did not deserve what had been happening to her did not make the pain go away.

"Why did Karl Greiner ever have to come here?"

Her plan was to keep busy until HR opened.

She went into Warren's (and Debby's) office "playroom" to leave a note for Debby to order three LOX tanks as soon as possible. She noticed several supply-issue sheets and computer print outs in the overflowing wastebasket. Instinct? Premonition? Whatever...

She took the papers and put them in her purse in a locker in the supply room until she could check to see if they contained pertinent information.

Ever since the computer commands had been changed without their knowledge, she had made it a habit to keep copies of everything she keyed to compare to Debby's revisions.

The person in charge of extended leave/retirement applications in HR was on vacation until the next Monday. Kay doubted she could stand it even that long, but she would try to tough it out since she wouldn't have Warren to worry about for one more day.

When Meryl arrived, Kay asked if she could explain why a ward alarm light was on but not theirs.

"If we needed oxygen, our light would be on," Meryl stated, but she refused to go with Kay to see for herself. Every time it was brought up, she would slough it off with a remark like, "It's working. It's working." Kay was deeply hurt by Meryl's attitude, but she still had a strong feeling Meryl was being forced to act against her will.

Roy Cooper, an electrician foreman, happened to stop in right after noon to use the phone. Kay asked if he would have a minute to check the oxygen alarm adding that it might be just a short or a burned-out bulb. If it did have a problem, it needed to be fixed.

Meryl butted in, adamant about keeping the

electrician away from the storage room. "That light is working, and it doesn't need to be checked," she insisted.

Cooper visited for a few more minutes and as he was leaving asked, "Where's that bulb you wanted me to check?"

Then Meryl got very upset. "It's working, and there's absolutely no need to check it. It's working."

When they started toward the door anyway, Meryl practically threw herself in front of the oxygen storage room door. "I'm telling you; it does not need to be looked at."

Kay gave up. "Just forget it, Coop, but thanks anyway."

When out of Meryl's earshot, he said. "I'll come back and check it for you later."

Roy was a nice man. He was the one Karl had stopped when he had tried to sneak extra electrical outlets into the education office for Kay.

She wondered what could have caused the one person in medical supply she thought she could trust to act like that. The only explanation was that Meryl had been threatened not to let anyone in that room until Warren could hook it back up.

Debby had still not ordered replacement oxygen tanks when Kay's shift ended so Meryl called the supplier herself.

When Kay tried to describe the way the oxygen room looked when the door was opened, Debby ridiculed her, practically called her a liar. Obviously short on knowledge of the three states of matter, she declared that "oxygen could not be seen."

That evening Kay googled some interesting

facts. *"Oxygen becomes liquid at -297F and stored at high pressure. When released into warmer air, it returns to the gaseous state – the same principle as water in a teakettle when it boils."*

At home Kay took the papers from the office trash out of her purse. The issue sheets were ok, but the printouts were interesting. It took her a minute to realize what she had. They were retrievals from programs to which only Warren had access with pull-up times ranging from 16:45 to 17:10 automatically printed on each page. That placed Warren in the institution after hours – 4:45 to 5:10 p.m.

The next morning, the alarm system was working perfectly. The three LOX tanks Meryl ordered were still full as were the four reserve units. Kay was relieved but extremely depressed that morning.

About 8 am, Meryl disappeared. Kay had no idea where she was until about two hours later when she saw her in Warren's office.

Just before noon, the associate warden called Kay to his office. He received a phone call just as she sat down across from him. While he talked, she could read a memo laying in front of him. It had Meryl's typewritten name on it but was not signed. So that was what she was doing in Warren's office all morning.

Kay could not believe what she was reading. She really couldn't. A full page of lies.

All she could say to Meryl when she returned was, "Why?"

"They made me write it," Meryl said. "I had to

do it over several times to get it to their satisfaction, just like before. They want to place the oxygen loss directly and totally on you. I only wrote out what you told me happened on tablet paper. I didn't see the final version. I guess Debby typed it; didn't even matter to them that I wasn't even here when you found it."

Kay thought she must be telling the truth as she had not seen any tablet paper with handwriting on it in the AW's office.

It was hard for Kay to comprehend how management was able to manipulate someone like that. Knowing what they had on her might have made it easier to understand, but Meryl would not discuss it.

As Kay left for the day, a self-satisfied Debby – who Kay was sure added in the lies on the typed page – had settled into the desk chair in the supply area with a large bag of popcorn. She probably stayed there until she decided to go home.

Monday morning there were more issue sheets on top of the office trash. Among them Kay found Meryl's original memo in her handwriting on tablet paper explaining that Kay had found the valve on the LOX tank open.

Meryl had written exactly what Kay told her happened just like she had said. With it was a typed memo with many notes written in the margins in Debby's handwriting expanding and beefing up Meryl's description. There was proof positive that Debby had written the memo and typed Meryl's name on it.

Kay knew what was coming. She needed help

from the union and soon. She made copies of all the evidence.

Union rep Rollie Alvarez, who was helping Tom, wondered why the low-grade clerk was so deeply involved.

"Pretty dumb, I'd say. Didn't even dispose of the evidence," he said.

Kay didn't seek their help any too soon because later that same day, She and Rollie were called to the nursing supervisor's office where Kay was given a "warning of unacceptable performance." It stated, in part, "You have performed your duties in an unsatisfactory manner by not obtaining oxygen before the system went on reserve." It went on to say she had not checked the oxygen resulting in what could have been a dangerous situation or possibly death if an emergency had arisen or patient needed oxygen after the hospital's supply was depleted.

"I'm supposed to check and order oxygen in the middle of the night when I'm not even here?!" Kay said after reading part of the document. She was aghast.

She turned to Rollie and said, "What about the dangerous situation and possible deaths created when the valve was deliberately turned on? I wonder if these people realize how ridiculous this all sounds."

The notice continued, "You are given 30 days to demonstrate acceptable performance and if you fail to accomplish this and maintain same in all elements during the remainder of the job rating period, you will be given an unacceptable rating which will result in reassignment, demotion or termination."

The notice then encouraged her to contact Warren or the nursing supervisor for assistance in performing her duties in a satisfactory manner – two of the last four people on earth she would ever ask for help or advice on anything.

Being rattled and not thinking coherently, Kay inadvertently left a page of Meryl's original memo in the copy machine. The associate warden's secretary found it, knew exactly what it was and couldn't get to Debby soon enough. Debby and her ilk then knew Kay and the union were on to them.

It was another one of those distinct "gut" feelings. But Kay did not heed the strong premonition screaming to take her purse with her when she left with the inmates to deliver supplies to the wards. The entire time they were gone, she had that haunting feeling about her purse.

Rollie came for copies of the memo and unsatisfactory notice later in the morning. She got her purse from the locked cabinet in the supply room. The copies were gone!

The thief also has taken her notes on the oxygen incident and copy of the 15-day suspension letter.

Luck, divine intervention, whatever... The person who had rifled through her purse had grabbed the thick bundle of copies but had missed the originals that were folded and in another section.

"No wonder they know every move we're going to make!" he exclaimed. "Nobody has the right to go through somebody else's private property. I bet someone has been going through notes all along. They just never took anything before – not until this time because these papers would convict them."

Everyone working in the medical supply area had keys to that locker, but only Meryl and Kay used it for their purses while on duty. The next day, Kay put hers in one of the visitor lockers in the front lobby and carried the key with her.

The office trash that had not been dumped for two months suddenly vanished and a shredder mysteriously appeared. They were not going to let Kay find any more evidence.

During her lunch break, Kay typed a memo to the investigative lieutenant reporting the theft of her personal papers. He met with her and Rollie later in the day and stated he would "investigate fully and get to the bottom of the matter."

Stress-related illness brought on by the ongoing sexual harassment, discrimination, sabotage, trumped-up charges and unfair disciplinary actions had already put Kay within a hair of a nervous breakdown. Realization of the possible dire consequences of the oxygen spill and someone going through her purse to steal documents was the last straw. She trusted the inmates working with her more than staff.

Kay made up her mind over the weekend that Monday morning would be her last day on that job. She told no one. Not her family, not Glenda, not Dan, not Tom or Rollie. No one. She had reached the breaking point; could take no more and was getting out while still alive.

As soon as she called the nurse supervisor, she

took her coffee mug and radio to the front and placed them in the locker with her purse.

She filled orders until 7:30 when the HR office opened. Hands shaking and voice quivering, she filled out the application giving the time of her doctor's appointment later in the morning as the time to begin her sick leave. She would go on "extended medical" and annual leave until it was exhausted, then disability retirement if approved by Civil Service.

Warren was back that day. Kay only caught glimpses of him in the hall, so much the better as far as she was concerned. He seemed happier than usual, must have been thinking about that big payoff.

During their investigation of Kay being accused of not maintaining the oxygen supply, Tom and Rollie found out a proposal letter had already been drafted to suspend her for 30 days. Prepared before the investigation even started, it was dated exactly 30 days after the unacceptable performance memo giving her that long to improve. Quality did not matter one iota. She was getting a month off cut and dried.

"I won't give them the satisfaction!" she said to herself.

She walked out vowing never to go back.

Kay did not know how long she sat in the car but realized her arm had fallen asleep on the steering wheel under her head. She gathered herself together, started the car and crept around the circle drive in front of One Building... away from her career.

CHAPTER 14

THIS IS THE BACK OF THE BOOK... DID WE WIN?

Kay had been on sick leave for six weeks – free of Karl and the hostile work environment – when the federal EEO investigator from Washington, DC, came to the institution.

About two hours into the probe, the investigator shook his head and declared to Tom, "I don't know what's going on here, but something sure as heck is!"

The investigation was thorough. Besides Kay's own affidavit, several testimonies "told it like it was." Even inmate memos were considered.

Management's stories were inconsistent. As in other hearings, three different versions described Kay's call to report the oxygen alarm on the ward, none of which were correct.

As correctional officers got too close for comfort regarding who was responsible for the deliberate near disaster with the oxygen, the director of nursing turned the rest of the investigation over to the correctional department.

Tom and Rollie learned that Nursing knew all along who had actually turned on the valve but were going to suspend Kay anyway to cover their butts. The matter was dropped entirely after she applied for extended sick leave.

At the end of the probe, the investigator provided Kay a copy of his completed report – two thick volumes containing every document since her saga began.

The EEO office ruled in Kay's favor and an attorney advised her that she qualified for Workers' Compensation because hostile conditions and/or environment at the workplace had caused her disability.

Medical Center management fought tooth and nail to prevent approval for those benefits.

Its response to her claim was a host of lies and misrepresentations. Every false accusation – all of which had been disproved or dropped entirely – was dragged out again and the institution steadfastly denied responsibility for her stress-related illness.

None of her honors or awards were mentioned.

Greiner's defense of his plots and discrimination against her was overkill, but nothing in his rationale addressed the harassment, false accusations or sexual innuendos and propositions he had made.

Kay learned of all those lies and denials when

she got a copy of her case file from the Federal Office of Workers' Compensation Programs.

But she prevailed in the end. Although the money from her favorable Workers' Compensation award was a lot less than her salary had been, she was glad to receive it when her sick leave and annual leave had run out.

She was not old enough nor had enough years in to receive full retirement, and it took about five years before she was awarded disability Civil Service retirement. It was based on her salary at the time she became ill which subsequently affects the amount of Kay's retirement annuity at age 65. About half of the initial retro payment went to reimburse Workers' Comp for what it had paid her in the meantime.

Her family was in dire financial straits. Their savings were gone, and some possessions had to be sold. Saddest and most traumatic time was when her husband and sons had to sell their cattle.

Karl and those who helped and/or protected him, had not only ruined a mother's health and career but had impacted her family as well. Kay's attorney considered letting the courts decide on a price tag. But how does one place monetary value on a trashed career? How much is financial security worth? Physical and emotional health? Human life?

Arbitration on the federal EEO case was held in Kansas City a few months later.

The arbitrator told Kay and her attorney that thousands of EEO complaints are filed by government employees each year. Out of each 100 complaints, only 12 reach arbitration. And, of those

12, only one will win and receive a monetary award. Kay's case was one of those. However, the settlement amount is limited by law to only a fraction of what the person should receive. It is also under a gag order.

After about five years, Kay finally recovered and went on to work as a newspaper reporter.

Kay tells anyone suffering through harassment or unjust punishment, seek someone who can advise on what kind of complaint is appropriate.

Then follow it through to the end.

CHAPTER 15

THE ROAD BACK

K ay was so insecure by the time she went on sick leave that she had no hope of ever becoming useful again. She had accumulated about two months sick leave plus about the same in annual (vacation) time. Her full retirement plans had included 20 years from the Bureau – same as military hazardous duty. The seven and a half from a previous federal position helped as it was added to her years in service.

Karl Greiner and those who went along with him cheated her out of a large part – about half – of her retirement.

"They might just as well take me out and shoot me," she told one of the doctors she was seeing during the first few months.

Kay did not have reoccurring serious suicide thoughts but experienced extreme depression and strong delusions of worthlessness. She felt she had no future in the work force; no one would ever hire her so she might as well just give up.

Reoccurring in her mind were versions of the devastation and loss of life that would have happened had a burning cigarette had been thrown under the oxygen storage room door when the room was full of leaking gas.

"You need to put all that out of your mind and don't ever let it back in," her doctor stressed during each visit. That was easier said than done though.

A prescription to help her sleep made her dizzy and sick to her stomach, so she quit taking it.

This doctor and Kay seemed to connect on the same level. He helped her to push unpleasant times aside and was instrumental in her recovery. He explained how to overcome her troubling belief she had lost several years of her life.

"Most important, don't dwell on the bad things or you will become bitter," he emphasized. "Especially don't think about time lost or things you should have enjoyed to the fullest. Just go back to the time before all this started and reset your mind and life there."

Then dwell in the present and live for the future. None of your good memories will be erased, but bad times will become dimmer and buried, he added.

She had a hard time accomplishing this mindset. Whenever she thought things were finally under control, something would happen to bring the cruel harassment to the surface.

For example, a few months later she was waiting at a stop light when Ben turned in front of her with Karl on the passenger side. Karl was glaring at her and Ben was smiling broadly.

Ben and Kay ran into each other at a store a few days later.

Karl was not at all happy," Ben said with a grin. "Seeing you ruined the whole rest of his day. His mood change was hilarious."

Laughing together was good for Kay.

Ben said, "I've heard a lot of people at work say that you are to be admired. You were the only one with the guts to stand up to him and stick with it."

Kay knew she could not have lasted so long if it had not been for the union, EEO and all the others who supported her.

Another time Kay needed to go to the institution to pick up some paperwork from Tom. While they were by the reception desk, who should walk in the front door but Karl. He spoke to the receptionist but ignored Kay and Tom. They found out why Karl didn't act too surprised to see them in the lobby when they got back to the parking lot.

One of Kay's sons, who had recently received his permit, drove her to the appointment and was waiting in the car. He told them that "some guy" had stopped behind the car as if studying it for a short time. He then started to move toward the front of the car but when he saw the kid in the driver's seat, he quickly spun around and continued to the institution door.

In answer to Tom's question, the teenager

described Karl to a "T" even the color of his shirt and tie. They knew Karl was nosing around her car until he saw her son at the wheel.

Tom stated, "In my 20 years as a union rep, I've never worked – or even heard of – a case like this." This was repeated by several union members. The above statement or something near to it was also stated by Kay's lawyer, the ULR investigator and the EEO investigator from DC.

Mortgage companies claim they will work with people when circumstances make it impossible to pay the monthly payment. This is not true of most companies. Kay wrote their mortgage company to explain and ask for time. They did not reply. But when the second month was due and still no Workers' Comp check in the mail, a registered letter came. It read that if payments were not caught up before the third monthly payment was due, they would begin foreclosure proceedings.

After Kay had been on Workers' Comp for about two years, she felt able to handle the last five of the 20 years hazardous duty with the Bureau needed to retire with full benefits.

She applied to return to work at the prison hospital in any position for which she qualified. But the warden – not HR – turned her down flat. The first few paragraphs of his letter touched on some of the false charges against her but not the exonerations. The oxygen incident was noted even though it was dropped after Kay went on sick leave and they knew someone else had opened the valves.

This warden was not involved in Kay's problem but replaced Warden Preston later and was the one represented by proxy at the arbitration hearing in Kansas City.

Near the end of the letter, he wrote, "You will never again work at any federal prison."

"That statement in writing alone seals us. We'll win any court action we may take. Talk about discrimination!" Tom exclaimed.

Of the warden, he added, "Tainted? You think? He's a coward and covering his rear because he knows they were all in the wrong. He wasn't even here when it happened."

Kay had still not discussed the harassment and the following fight for justice with anyone except those involved in the struggle. Her husband knew she was appealing something that happened at work but knew nothing about the cases. He was allowed to sit in on the arbitration hearing during which his facial expressions clearly confirmed he was hearing it all for the first time.

When asked by the arbitrator if he had anything to add to the testimony, he replied, "I remember one morning when she was getting ready for work, she said, 'I'd give anything in the world if I didn't have to go out there today.'"

A few years later Wayne Robbins of HR asked a family member who was then working at the medical center if he knew anything about why Kay resigned. The reply was that he only knew she got sick and had to quit.

"She was one of the most professional people I've ever met," said Wayne. "She never discussed the problem with anyone outside the Bureau even her own immediate family."

He went on to explain that Karl was a micro-manager with severe interpersonal problems, especially with women. He had no conscience, scruples, ethics nor integrity. He was sinister, domineering and disturbed to the point of being cruel.

Approval for Workers' Comp or disability retirement seem to take an eternity. Kay anxiously checked the mailbox each day with anticipation. One day after again finding it empty, she erupted into tears on her way back to the house.

"I just can't do this anymore," she said aloud. "I just can't... I give up...don't care what happens to me anymore," she sobbed. "What else can I do?"

At that point she gave up and turned the entire "mess" over to God and cried out for help.

She didn't realize it at the time but not long afterward, she realized that was the point she began to feel better. Shedding it off her shoulders felt like a ton had been lifted off her back. It was unbelievably wonderful. She was surprised she could pinpoint that exact time as when feelings of despair and sadness started to change.

She felt energized again and began to seek a writing job – something she had wanted to do since childhood and her business degree had encouraged. After several months of research, calls, letters, rejections and disappointment – but most of all perseverance – she landed a job with a small-town newspaper. She soon moved on to a county paper, then a regional magazine and finally her dream job – reporter at a nationally circulated city daily newspaper.

Kay credits writing *Targeted Innocent* as therapeutic and having a large part in her recovery. She hopes it will help others going through similar experiences.

EPILOGUE

Kay Richards fully recovered from the stress-related illness and subsequently earned a computer office management degree, tuition paid by Workers' Compensation. She now is enjoying her second career – writing and reporting for newspapers and magazines. *Targeted Innocent* is her first book.

Dan Williams retired about two years after Kay. He described his first day of retirement as "the happiest day of my life."

Also retired are those who helped Kay survive Greiner's vicious harassment including Tom Hilton, Glenda Potter, Rollie Alvarez, Ben Byerly, Meryl Simms and others.

Civil Service employees of the Dept. of Justice, Bureau of Prisons, are eligible for hazardous duty retirement (like military) after 20 years of service. Retirement age is usually 48 to 50. Any additional civil service employment is added to the above.

Wayne Robbins later became openly at odds with Karl Greiner and regretted the part he had played in Kay's ordeal. He became ill while in his early 40s and had to take a medical retirement.

Earl Norman received his coveted promotions and was transferred at least twice – to Oklahoma, then California. No one has heard but he is assumed to be retired.

Warren Crowe suddenly quit the Bureau, as did his nurse wife, soon after the oxygen incident. He left a forwarding address in California, but EEO and other investigative officers were unable to locate him for an affidavit. The union learned he was told to resign or be fired.

Debby Milford was moved to medical records, kept busy and supervised. No other information about her is available.

Karl Greiner received no reprimands from superiors and retired with full benefits. He then worked for a short time at a local halfway house. The supervisor there had been corrections department head at the medical center and was aware of Karl's treatment of Kay. He had also overseen the oxygen incident investigation. The union learned that Karl was fired from the halfway house, because he kept pulling the same shenanigans as at the medical center. For example, he kept saying, "Let's fire this one or that one" or "We need to fire him or her." Finally, the supervisor became fed up with Karl's harping, and said, "You know what... I'm just going to fire you." Karl died in 2012.

Targeted Innocent is a true story. Fiction was used for continuity in a few places. All names are fictitious to protect the privacy of all involved.

This book can be used as a guide to anyone going through a similar experience and also provide encouragement.

ABOUT THE AUTHOR

Donna Baxter began her professional writing career by freelancing for several magazines including Ozarks Mountaineer, Springfield! Magazine and Cat Fancy.

She was then employed by two county weekly newspapers and Springfield! Magazine. Next she enjoyed 15 years as a reporter and features writer at the Springfield, Missouri, News-Leader, a nationally circulated daily.

Before her writing career began, she was employed by three government agencies. This included 13 years at the Medical Center for Federal Prisoners in Springfield, Missouri where Targeted Innocent happened.